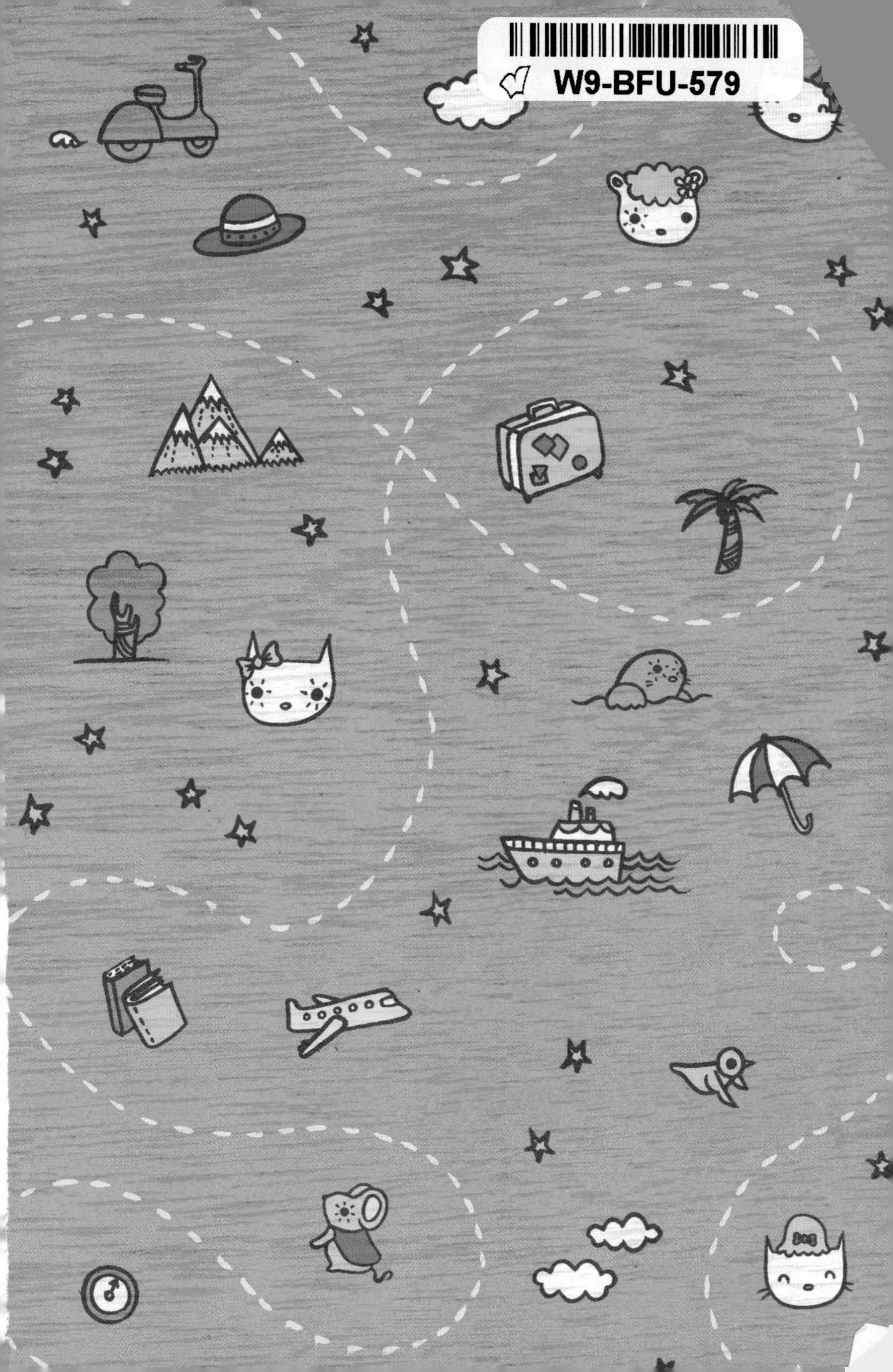

HELLO KITTY®
Here We Go!

stories and art by
Jacob Chabot and Jorge Monlongo

hello kitty shorts by
Susie Ghahremani

HELLO KITTY
Here We Go!

Stories and Art Jacob Chabot and Jorge Monlongo
Endpapers and Shorts Susie Ghahremani

Cover Art Jacob Chabot
Cover and Book Design Shawn Carrico
Design Support Kailash Black
Editor Traci N. Todd

Printed in China

Published by VIZ Media, LLC
P.O. Box 77010
San Francisco, CA 94107

10 9 8 7 6 5 4 3 2 1
First printing, October 2013

Stories and art by Jacob Chabot:
"Deep Clean," "Breezy Does It," "Lunch Date,"
"Watch the Birdie," and "Turn the Page"

Stories and art by Jorge Monlongo:
"First!", "Super Spy" and "Back in Time"

Stories and art by Susie Ghahremani:
"Moonwalk," "On the Road" and "Bear Attack"

PARENTAL ADVISORY
HELLO KITTY: HERE WE GO!
is rated A and is suitable for
readers of all ages.
ratings.viz.com

Contents

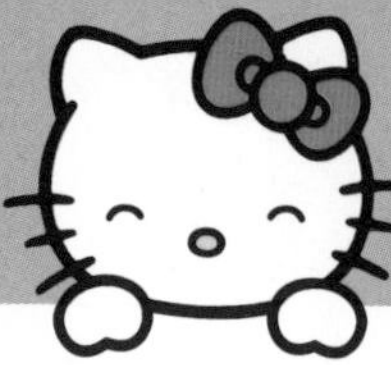

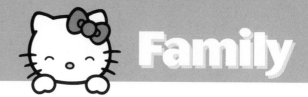

Family

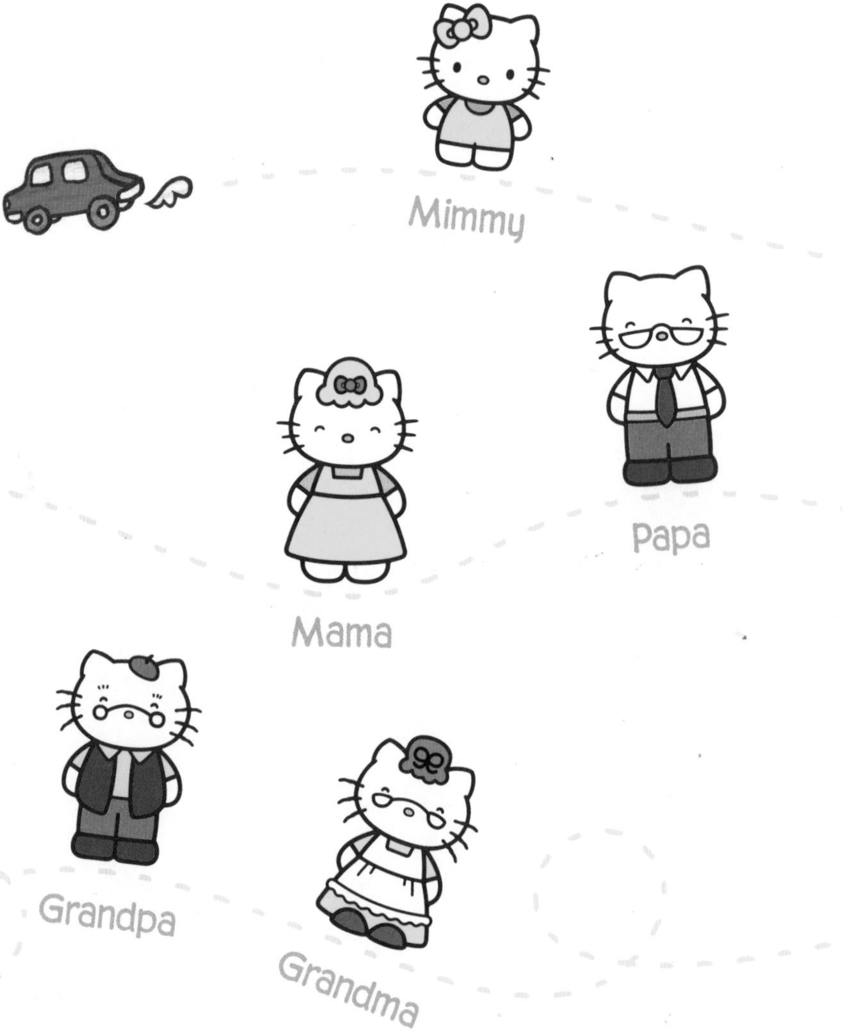
Mimmy
Papa
Mama
Grandpa
Grandma

and Friends

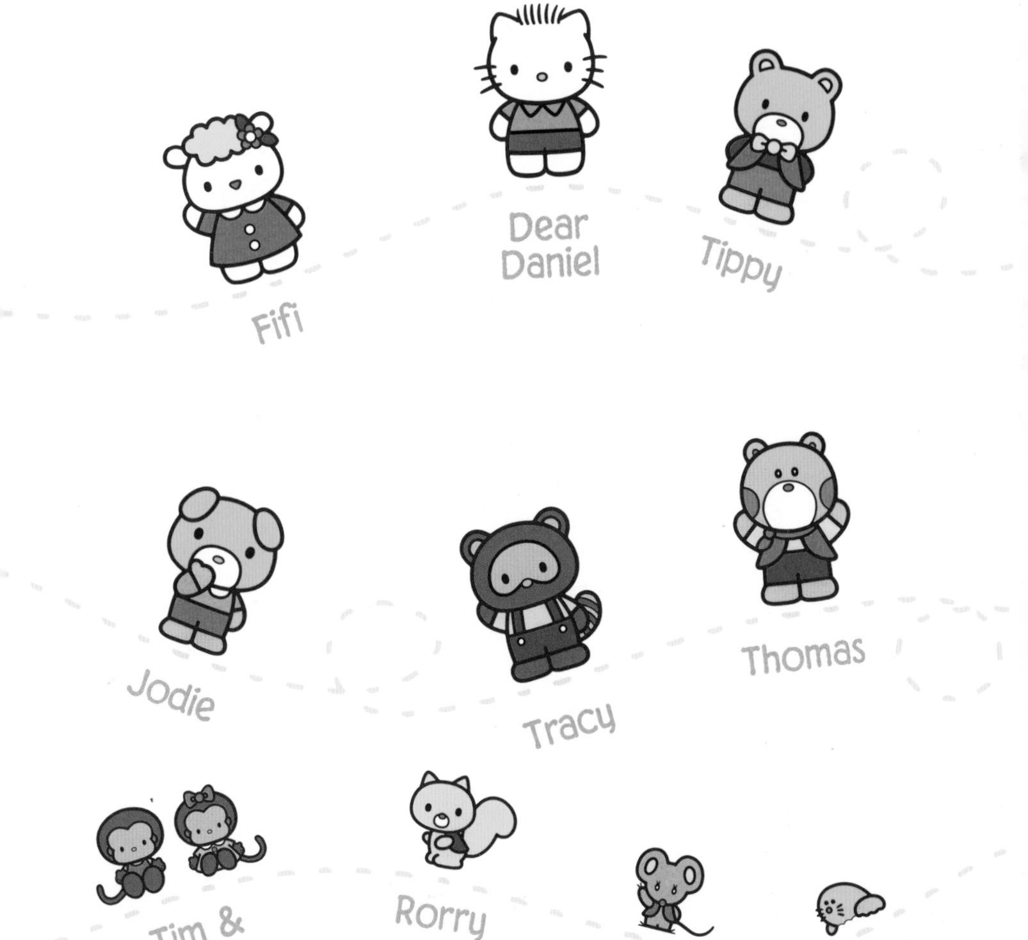
Fifi
Dear Daniel
Tippy
Jodie
Tracy
Thomas
Tim & Tammy
Rorry
Joey
Mory

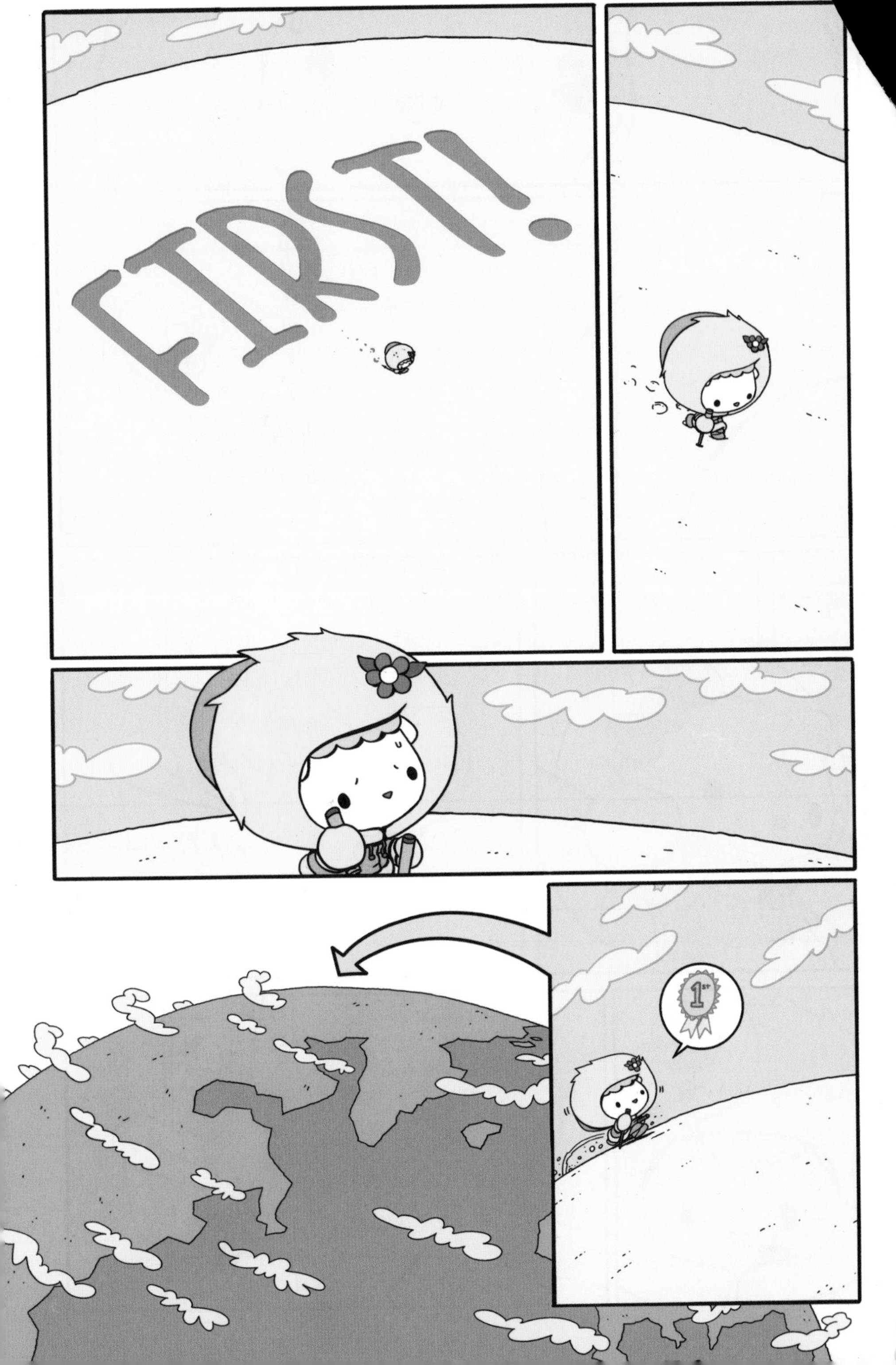
FIRST!
1st

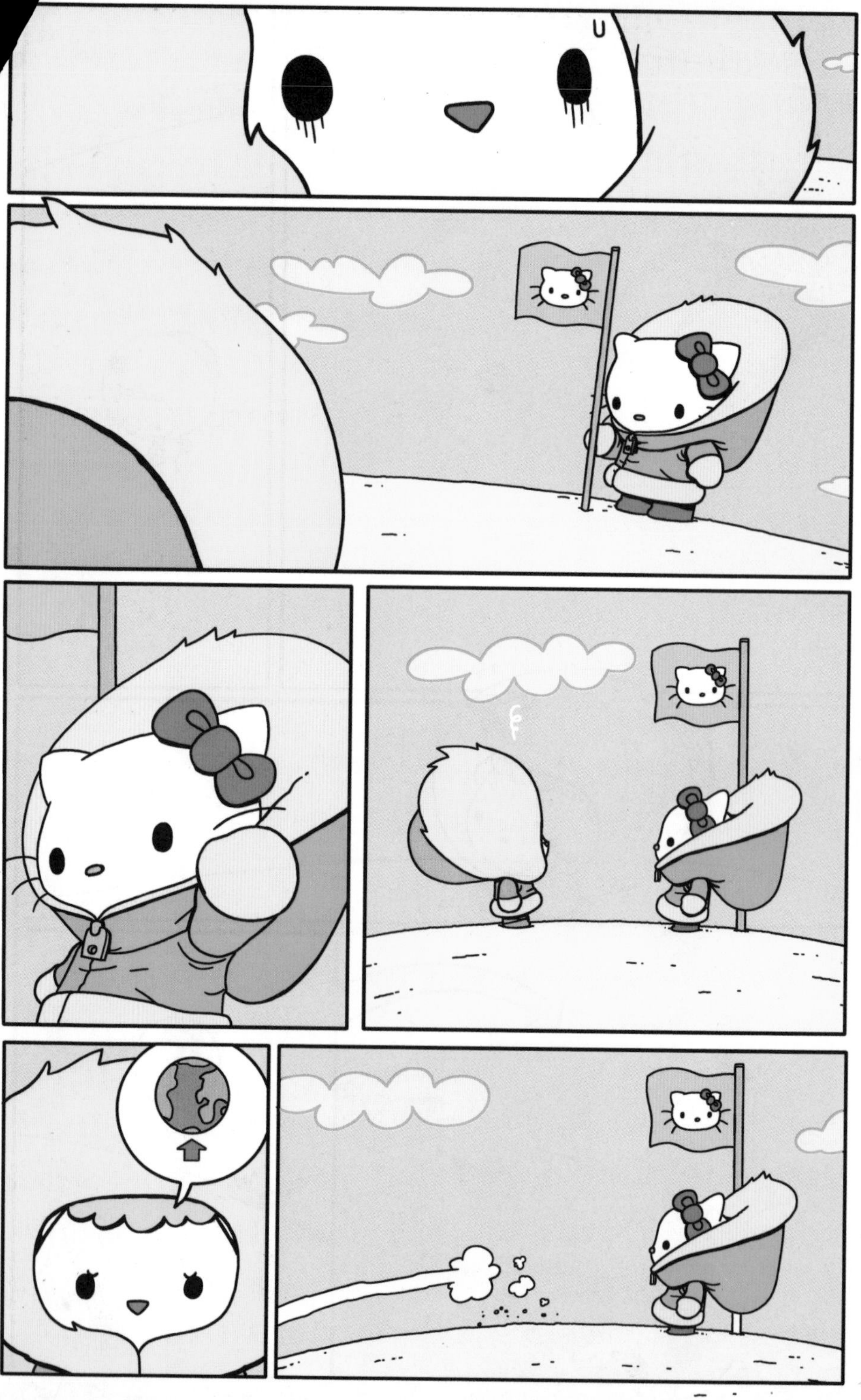

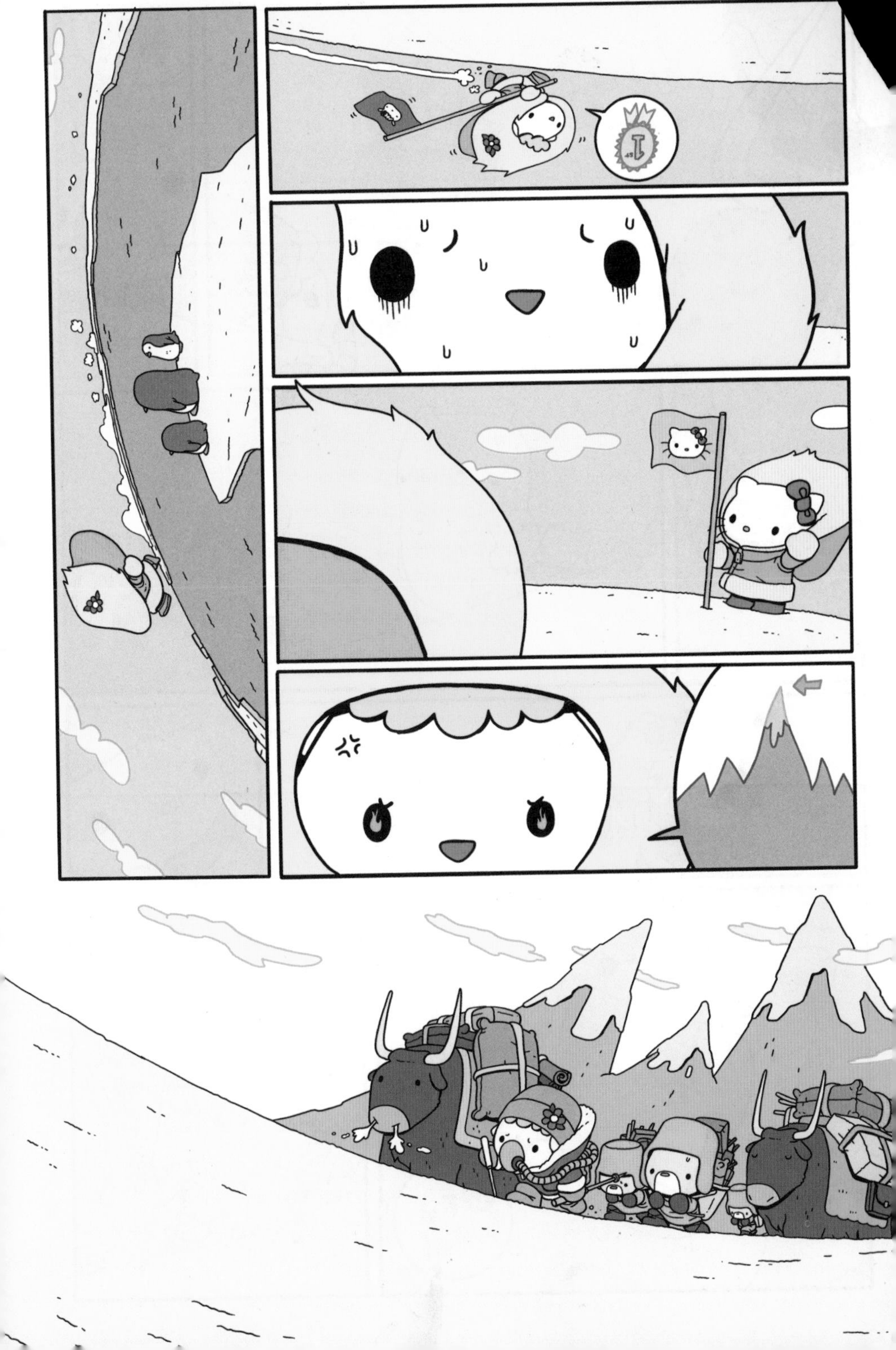

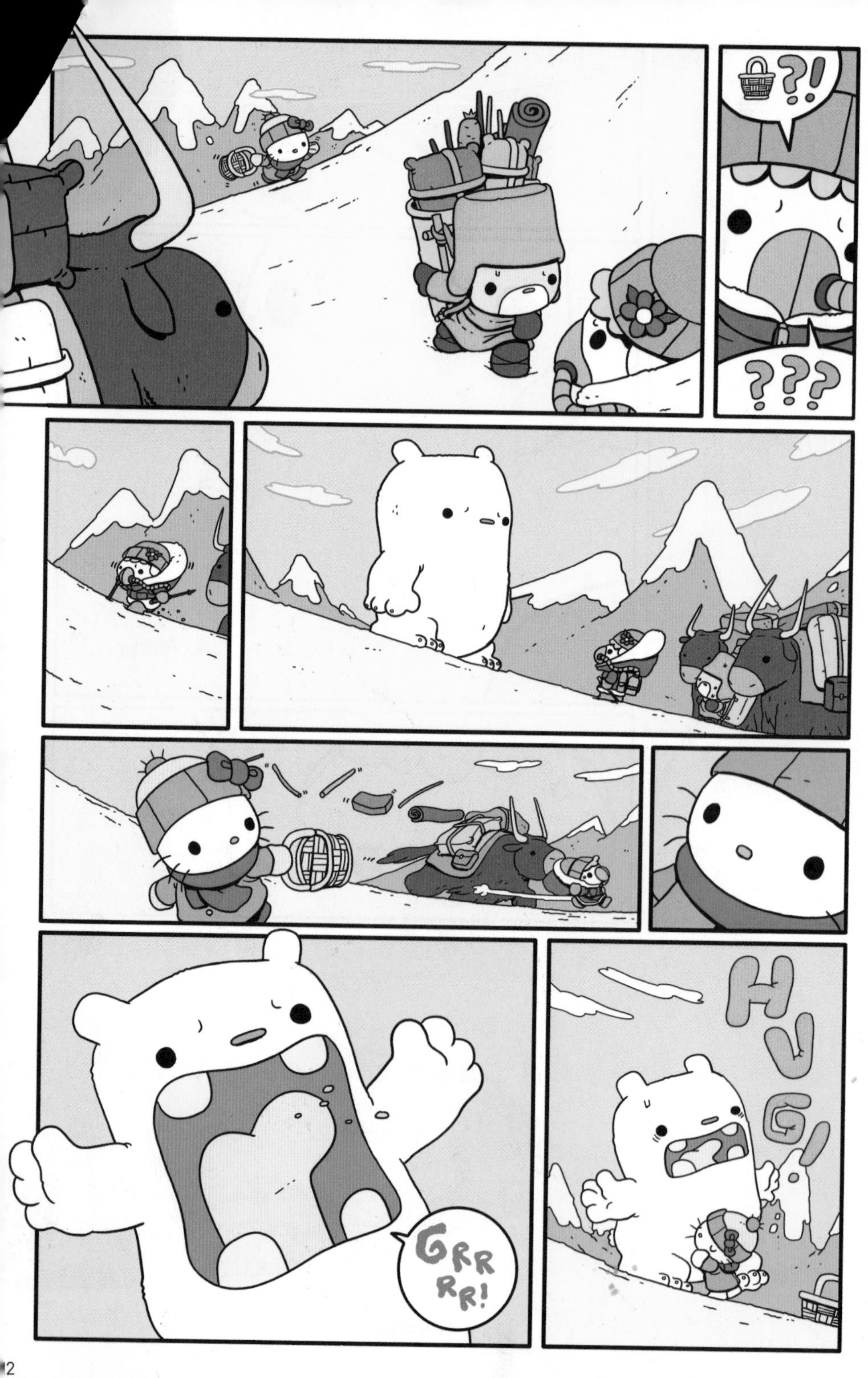
?!
???
GRRRR!
HUG!

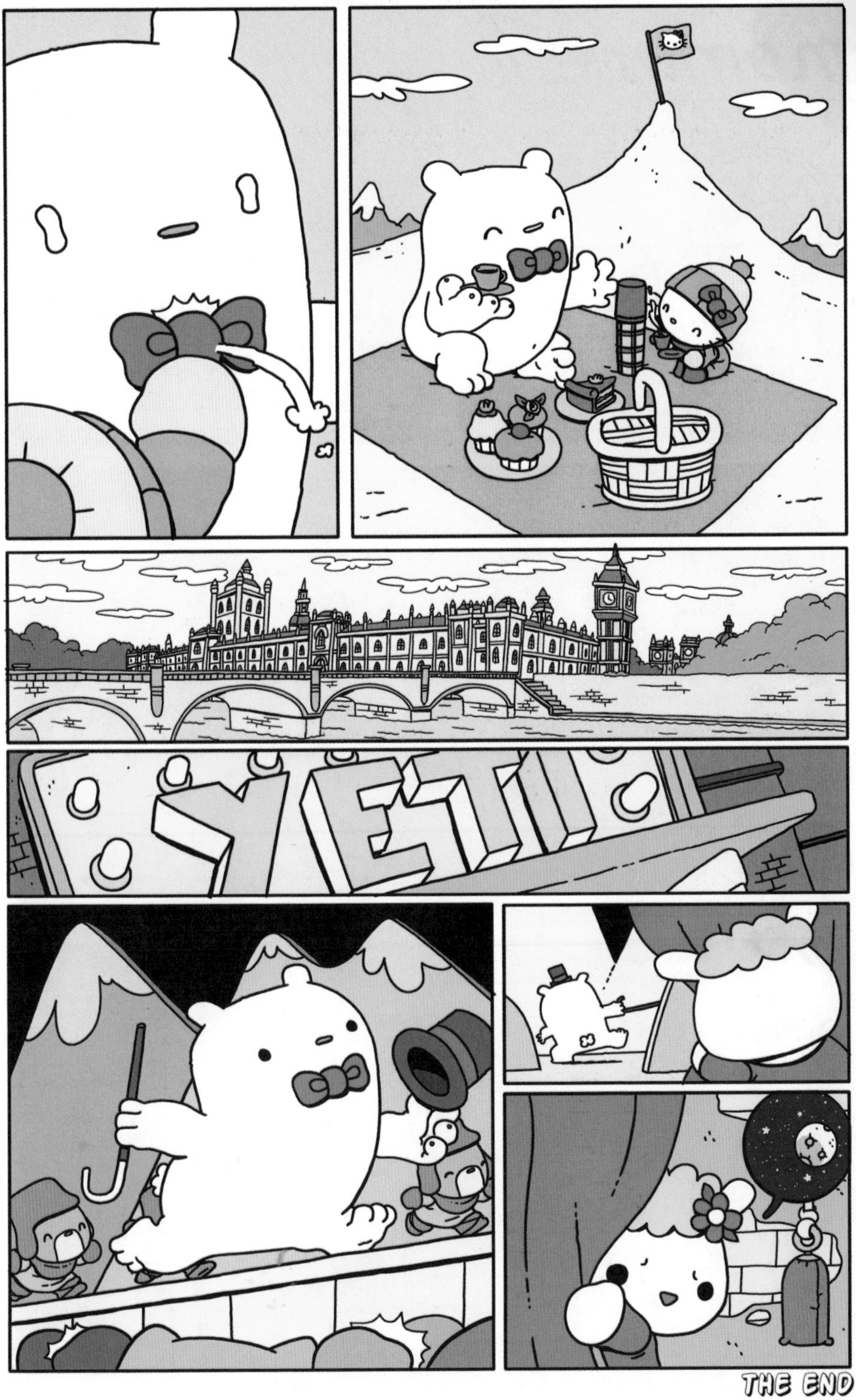

YETI

THE END

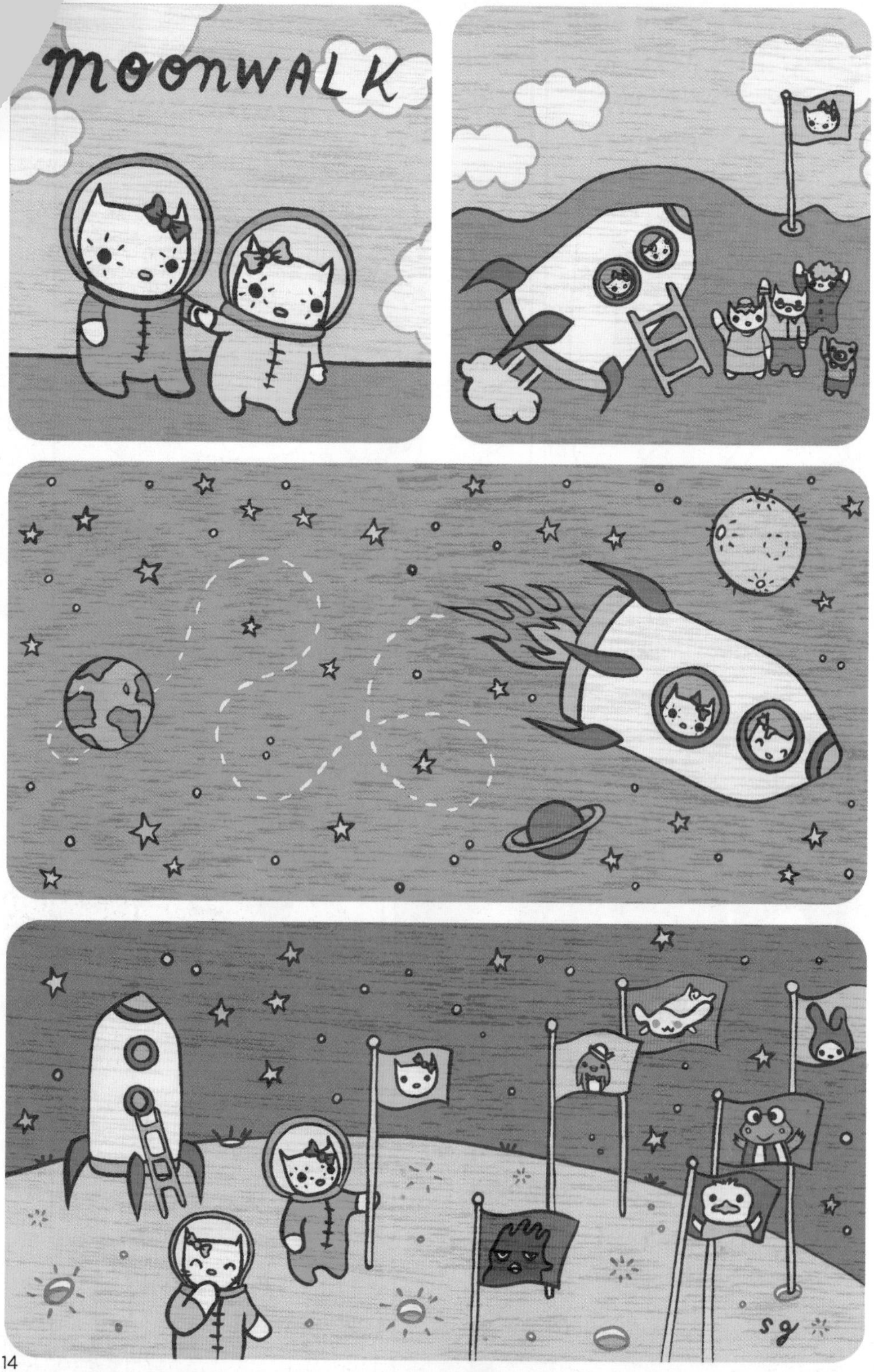

MOONWALK
sg

DEEP CLEAN

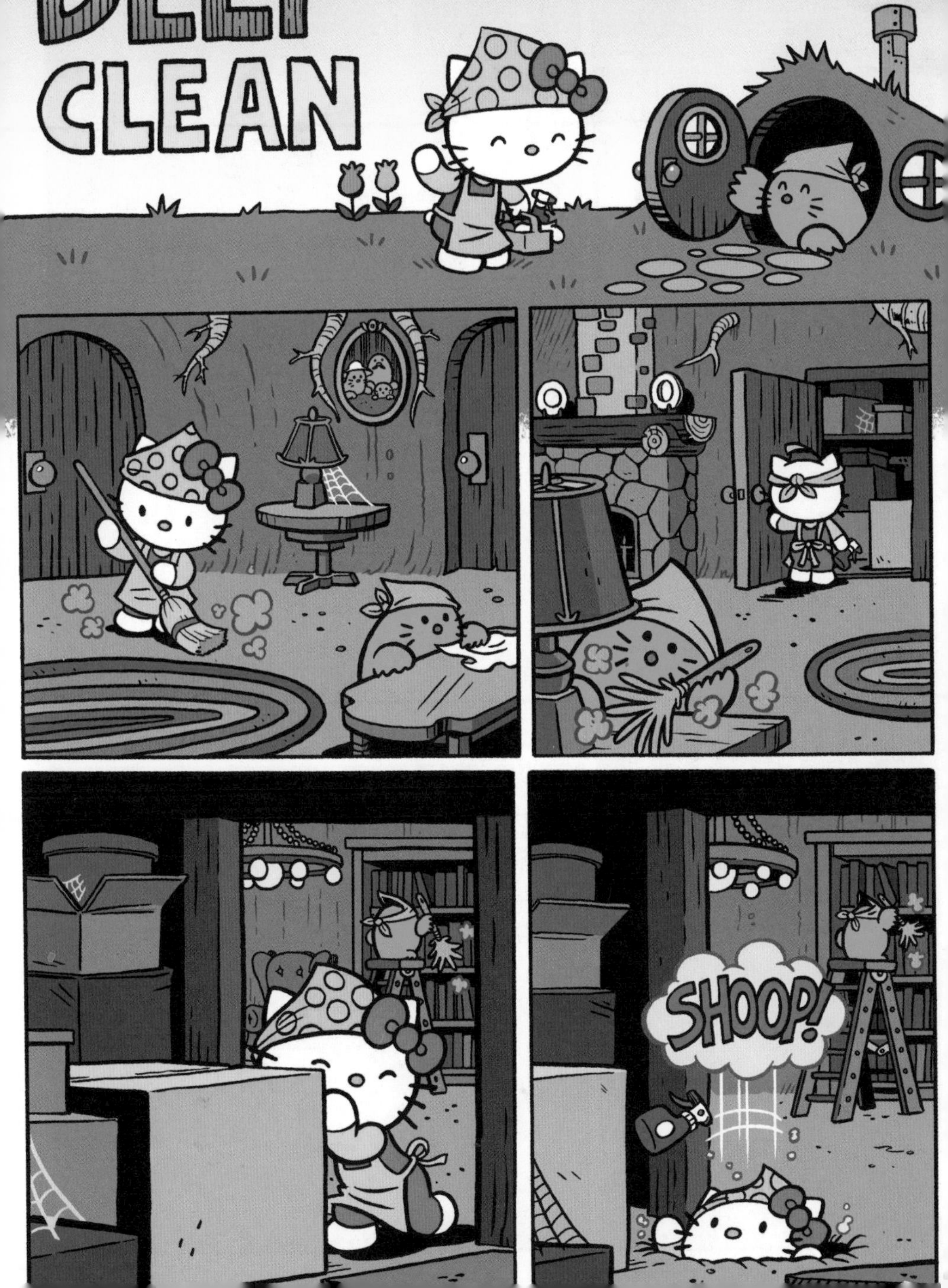
SHOOP!

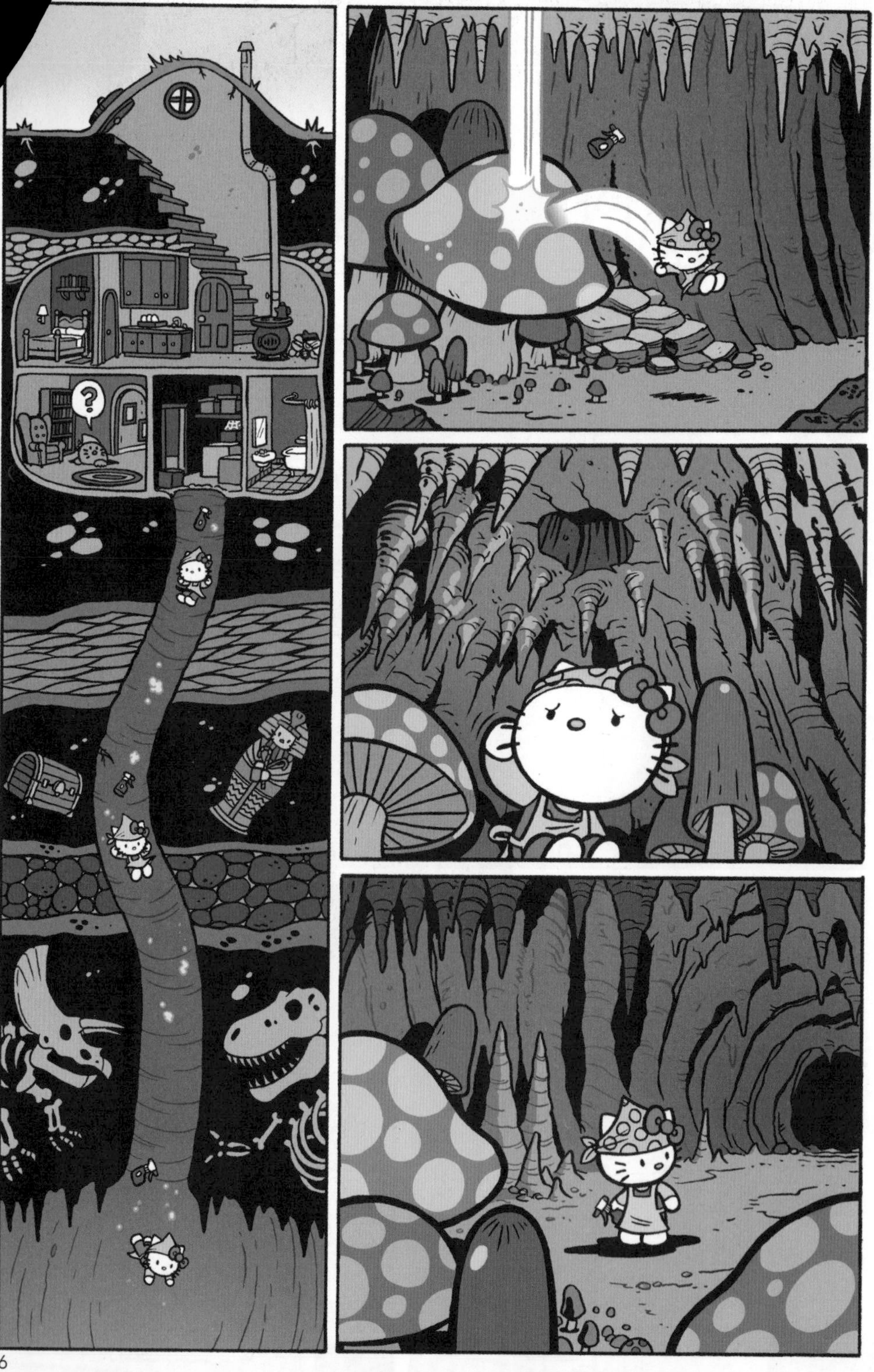
?

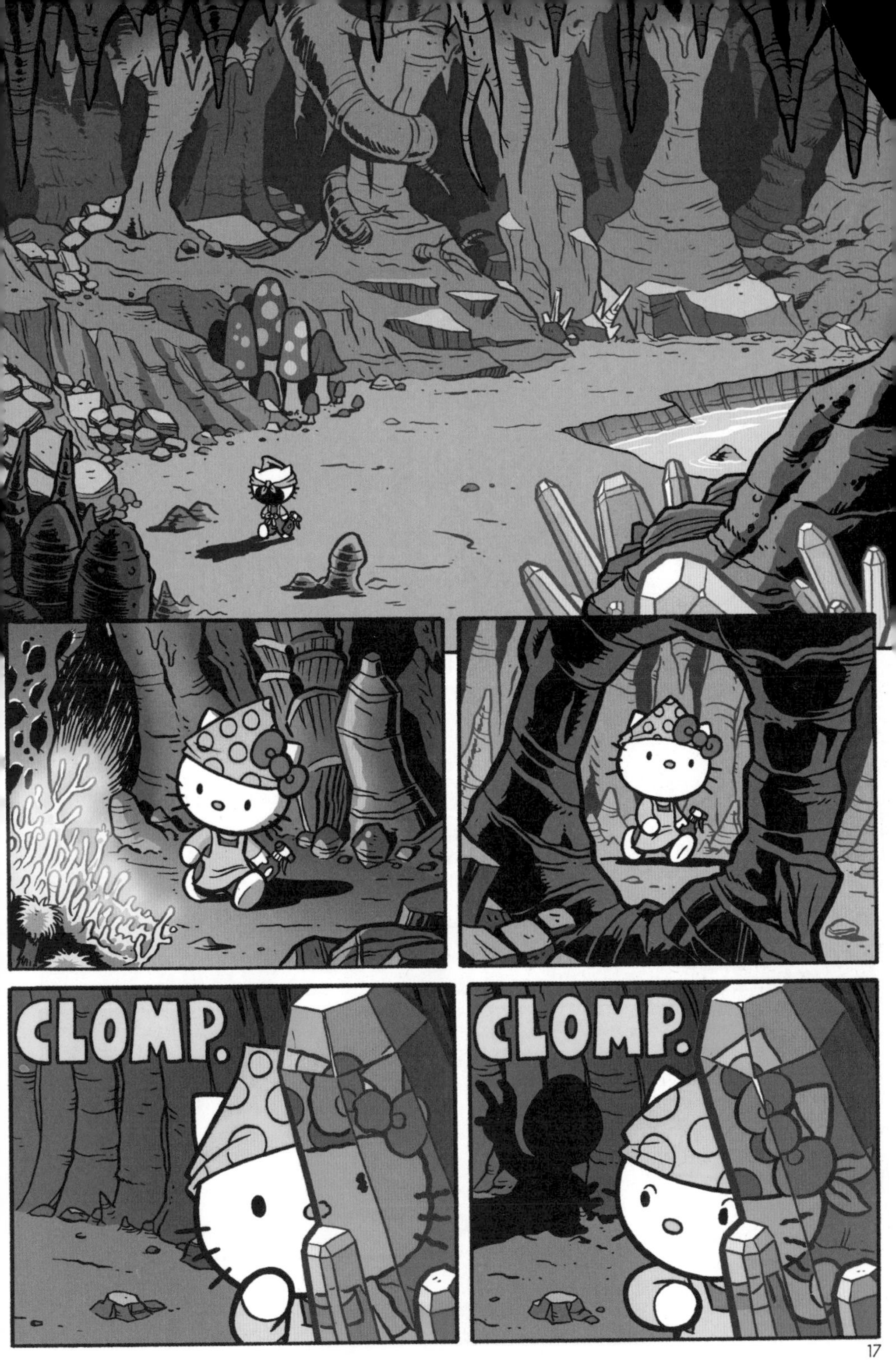
CLOMP.
CLOMP.

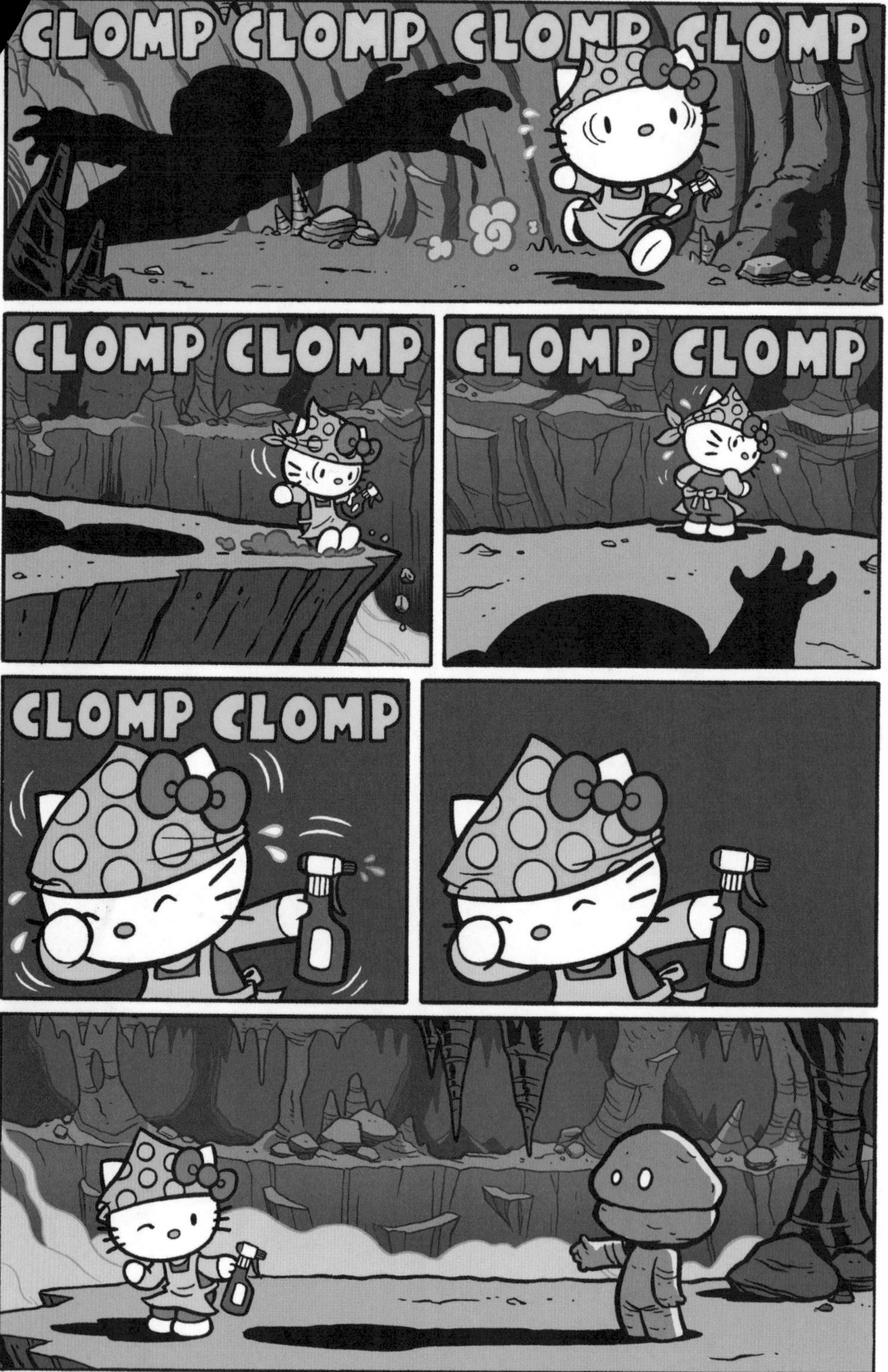
CLOMP CLOMP CLOMP CLOMP
CLOMP CLOMP
CLOMP CLOMP
CLOMP CLOMP

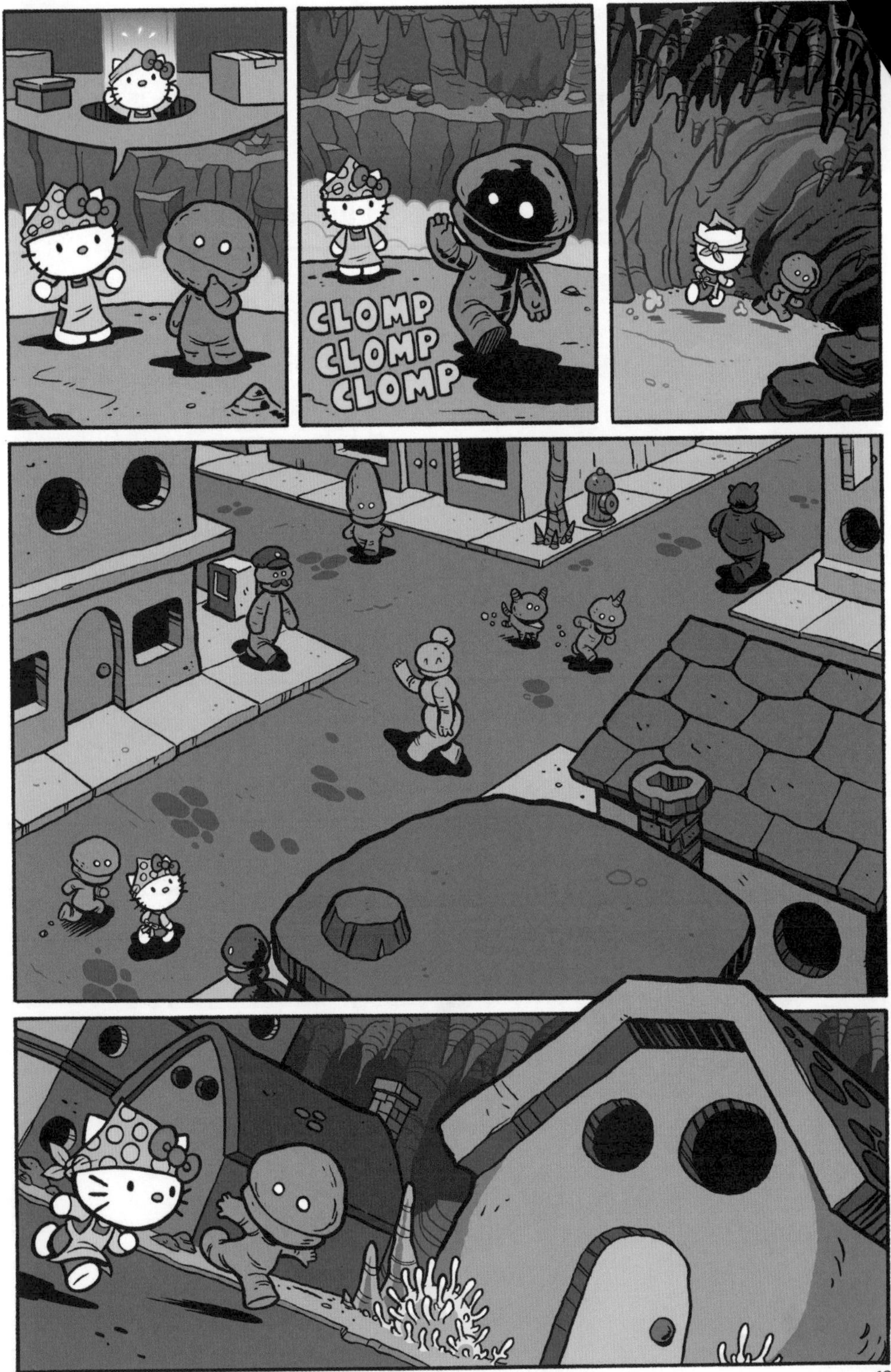
CLOMP
CLOMP
CLOMP

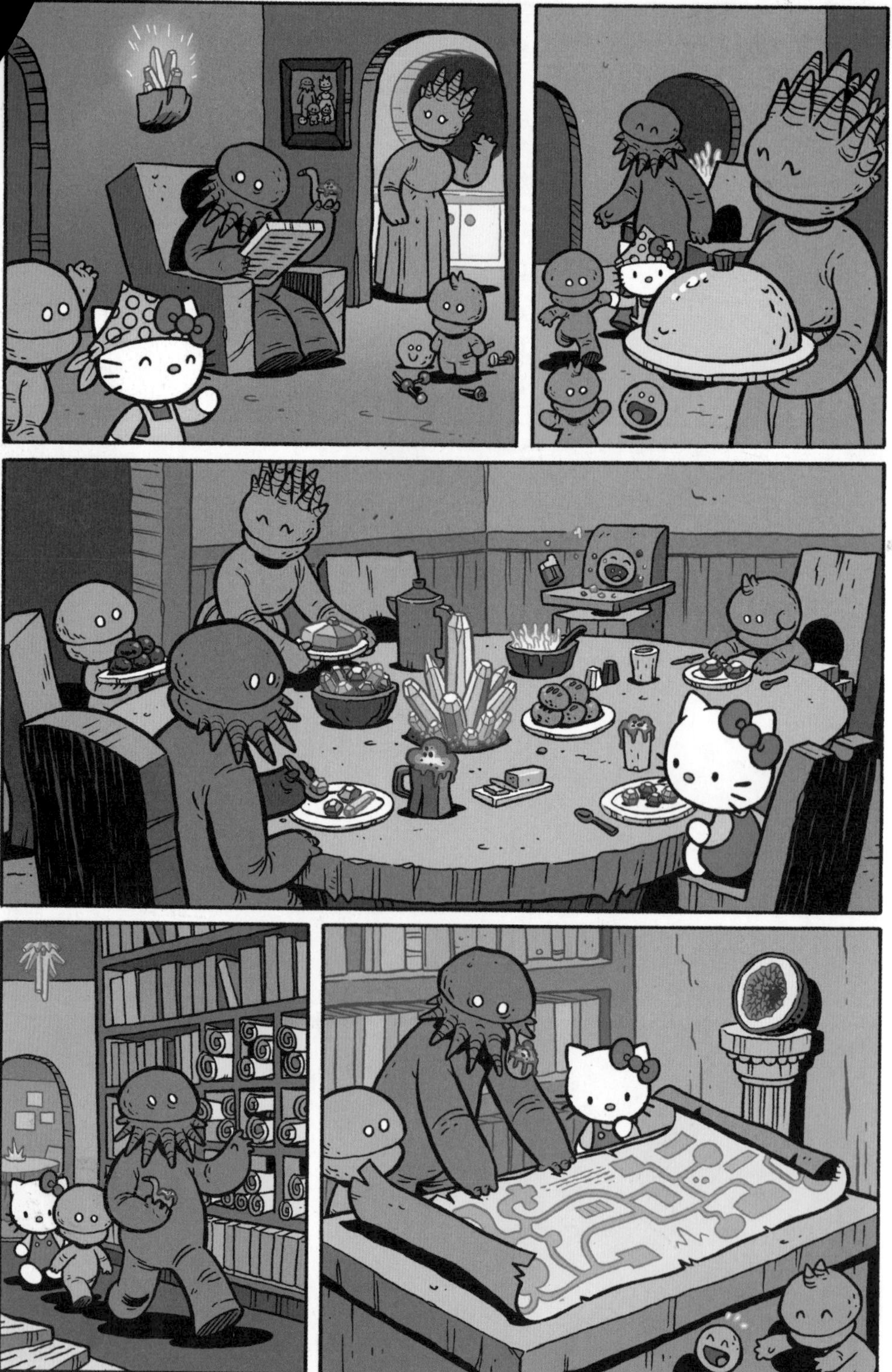

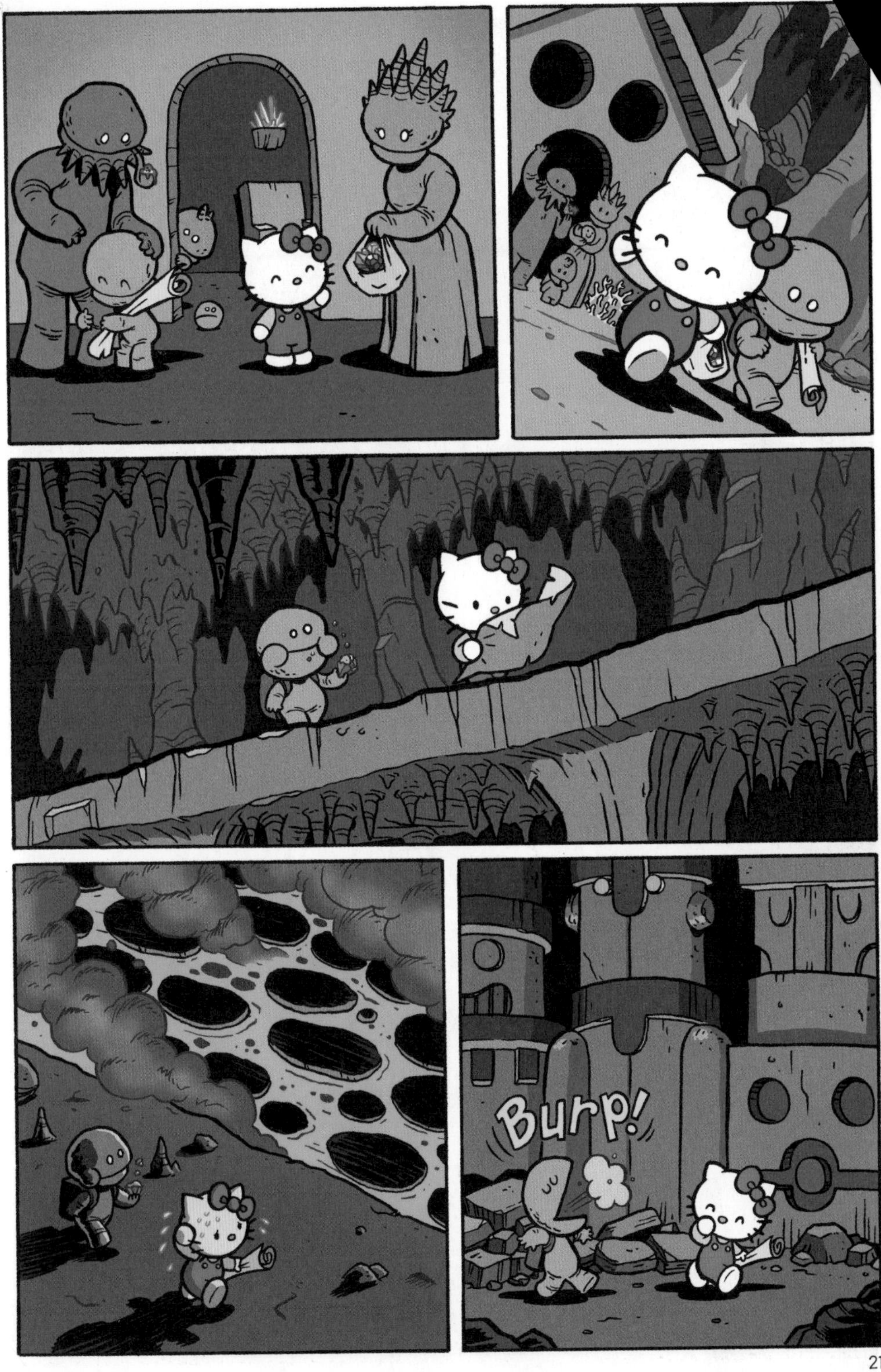
Burp!

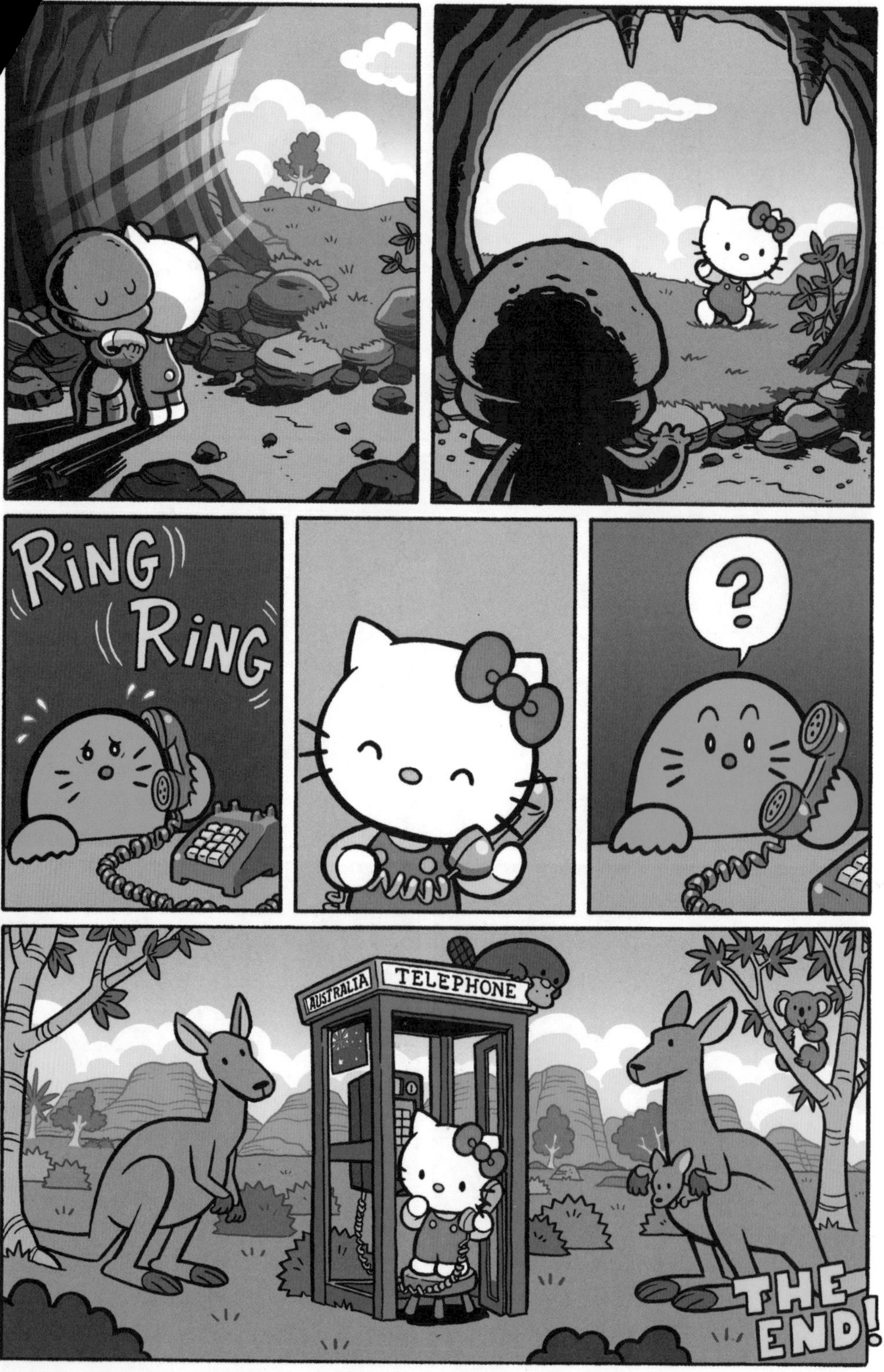
RiNG
RiNG
?
AUSTRALIA
TELEPHONE
THE END!

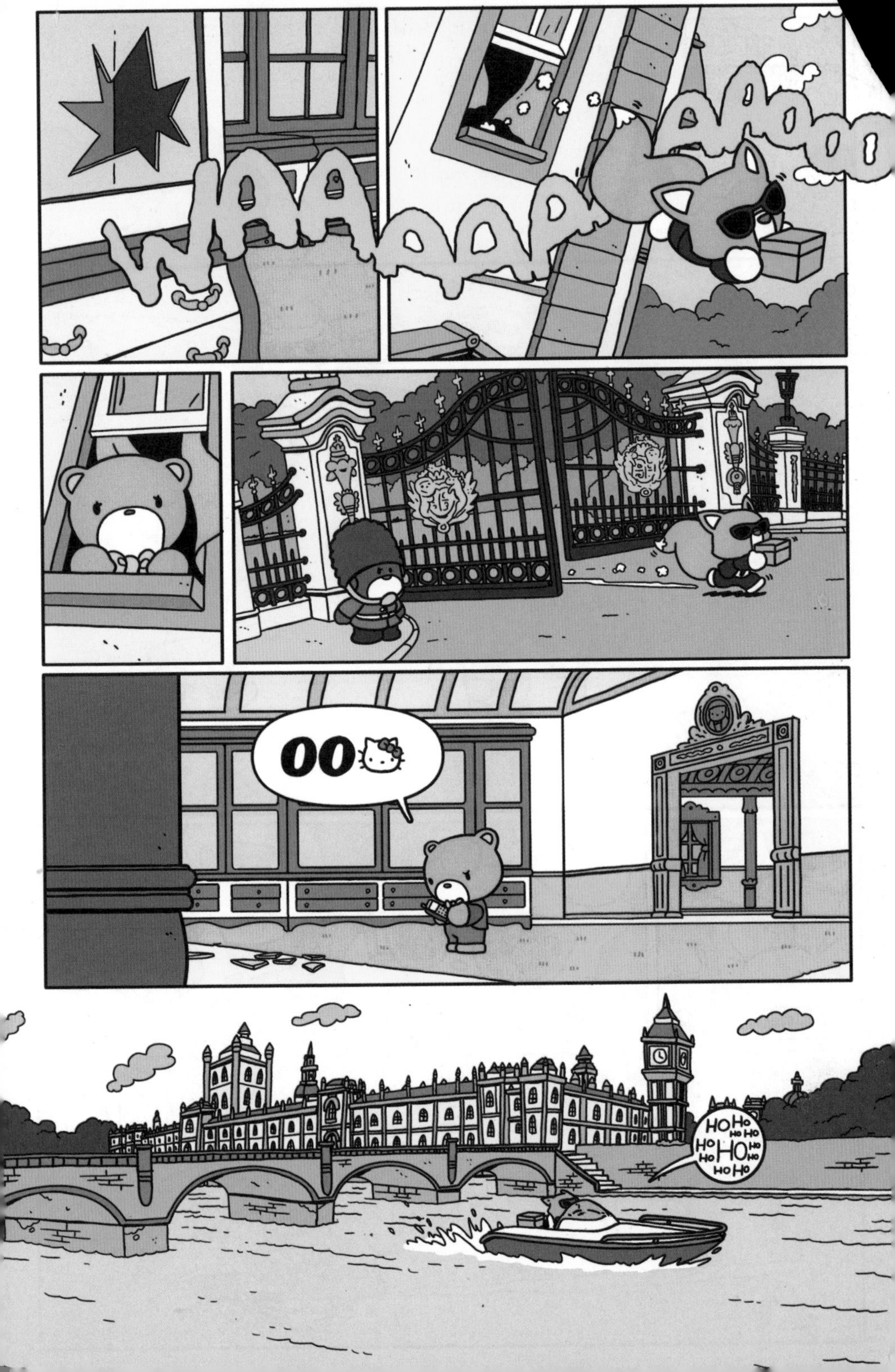
WAAAAAAAAAOOO
00
HO Ho HO HO
Ho HO HO HO HO HO
HO Ho

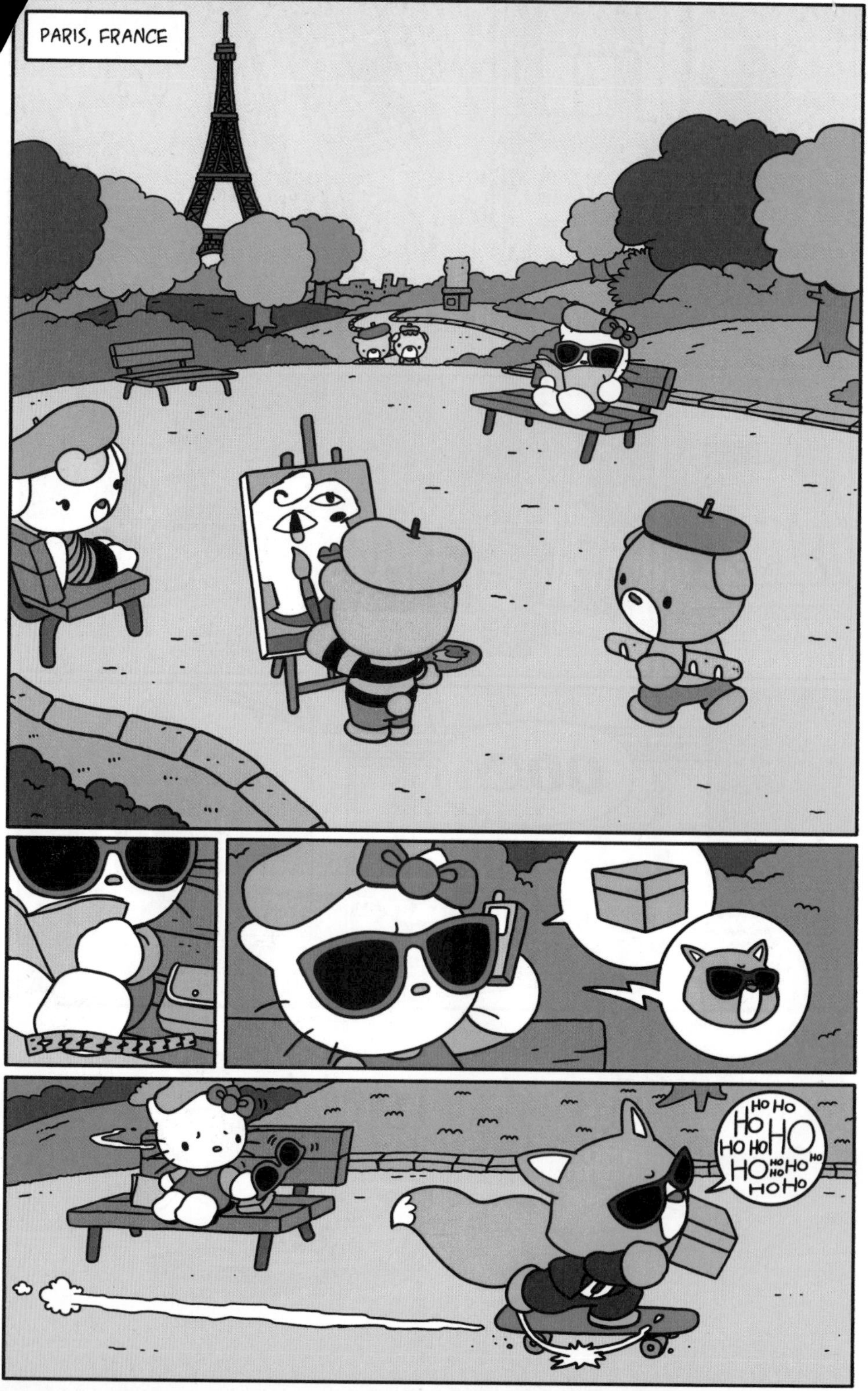
PARIS, FRANCE
BZZZZZZZZZZ
HO HO HO HO HO HO HO HO HO HO HO HO HO HO HO

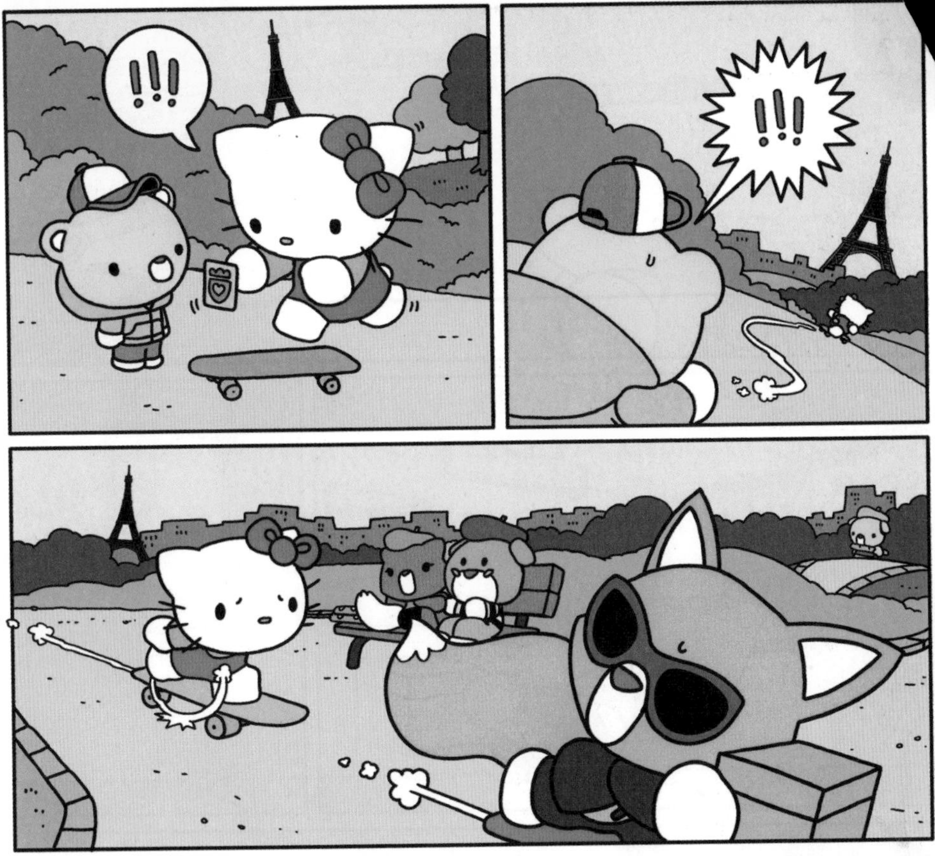
!!!
!!!

SUPER SPY

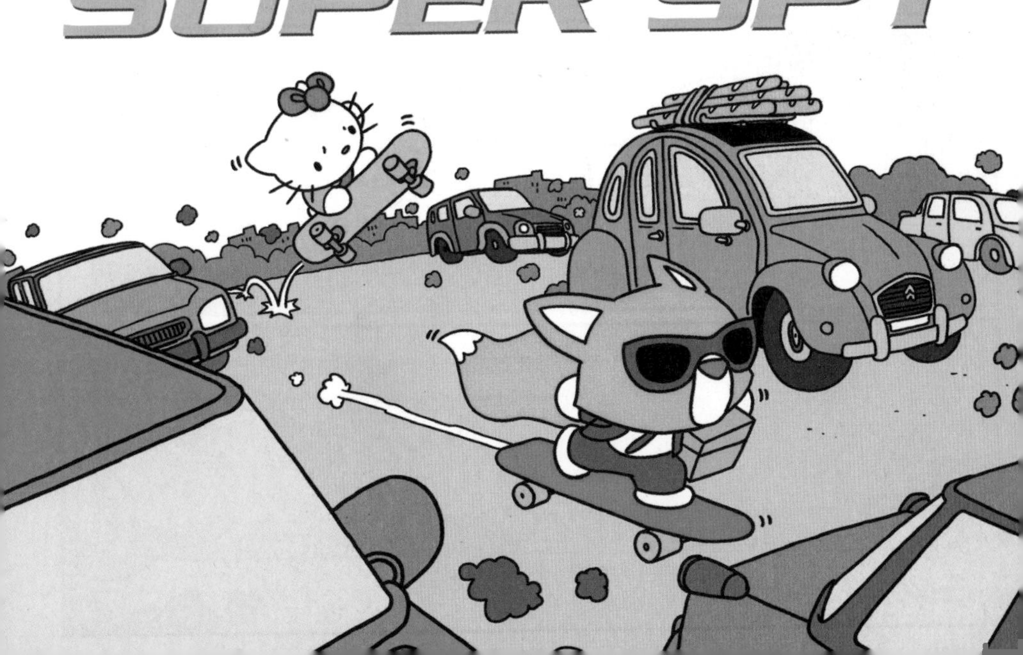

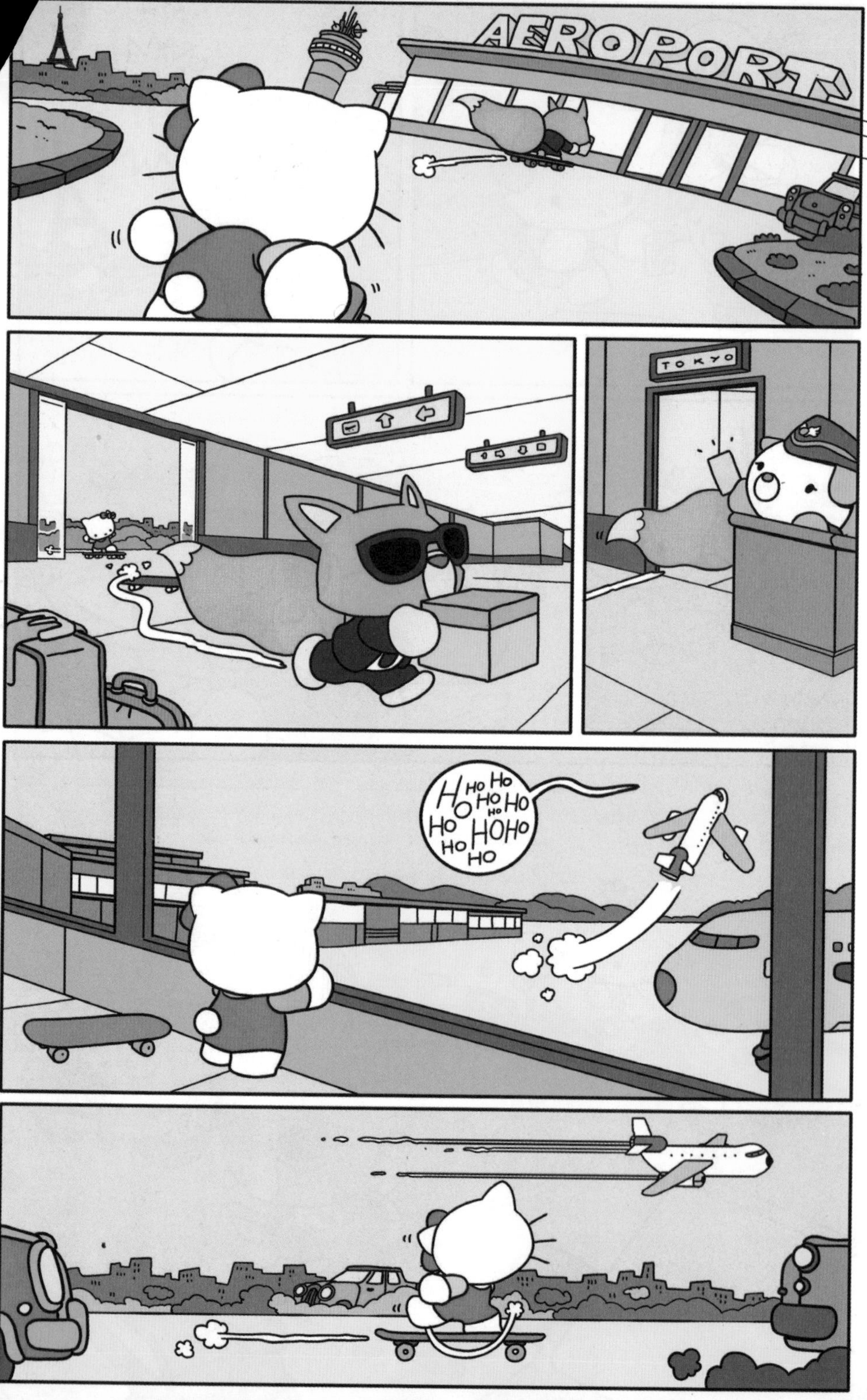

AEROPORT
TOKYO
Ho Ho Ho Ho ho Ho Ho Ho HOHo Ho HO

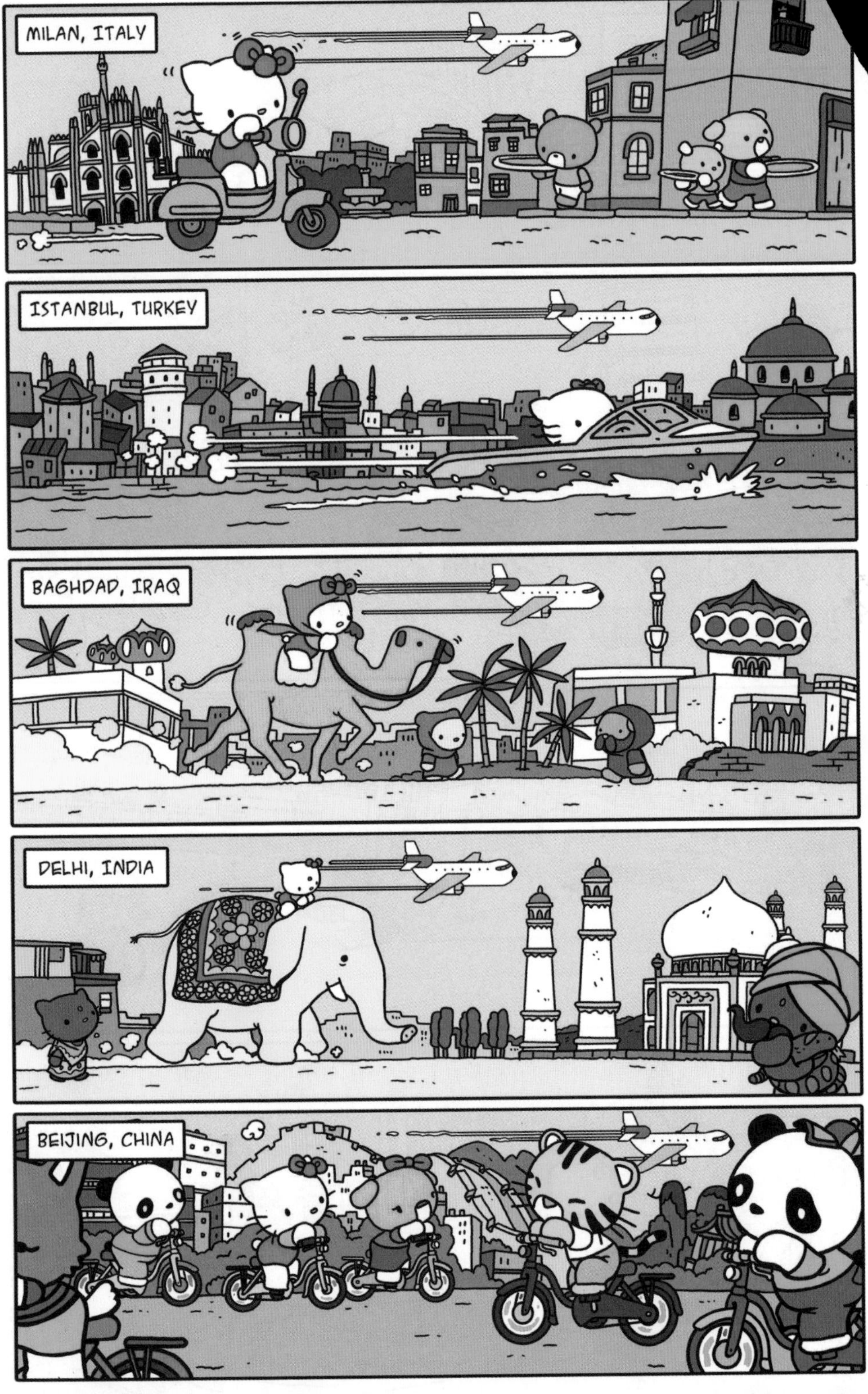
MILAN, ITALY
ISTANBUL, TURKEY
BAGHDAD, IRAQ
DELHI, INDIA
BEIJING, CHINA

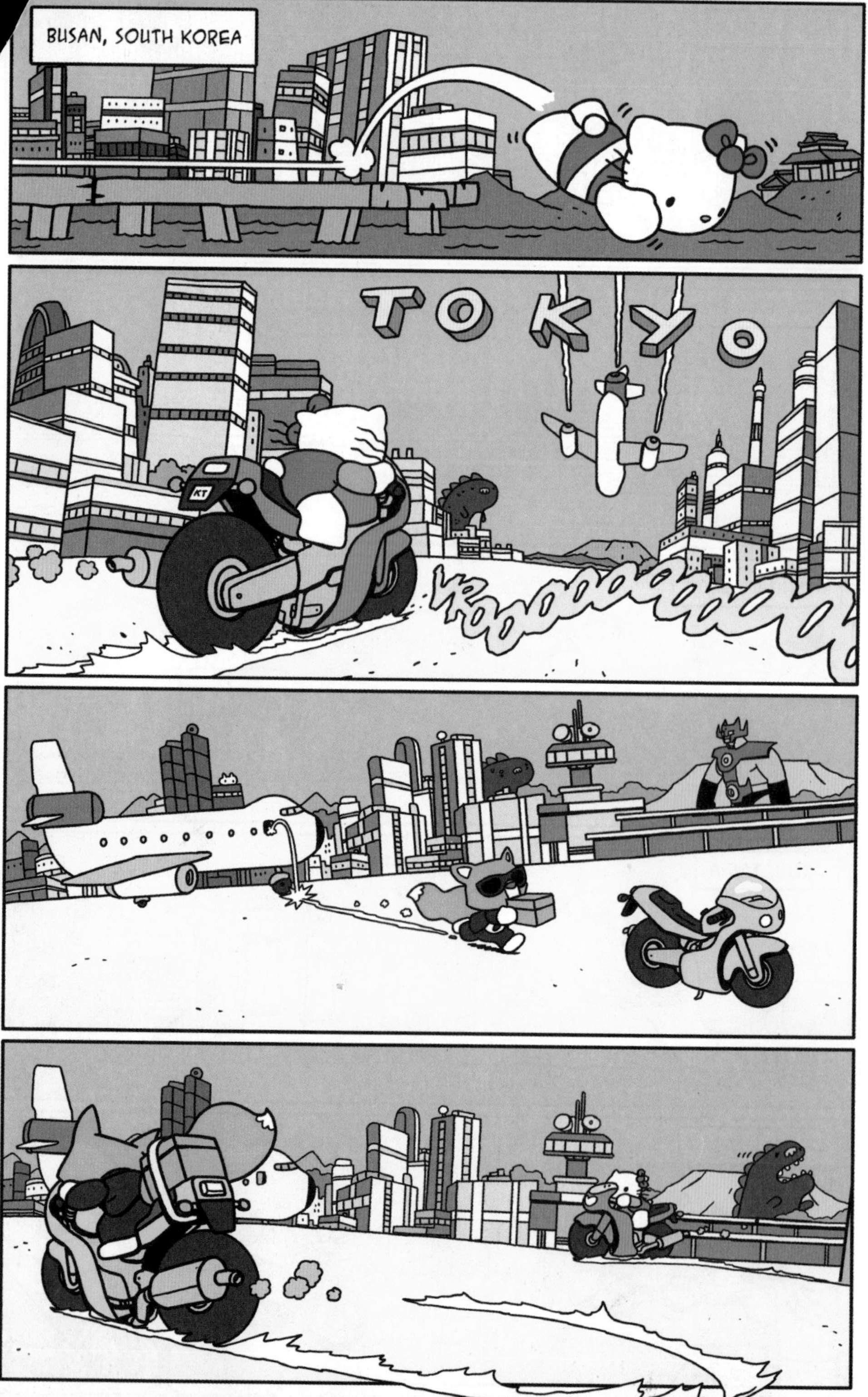
BUSAN, SOUTH KOREA
TOKYO
KT
VROOOOOOOOOOM

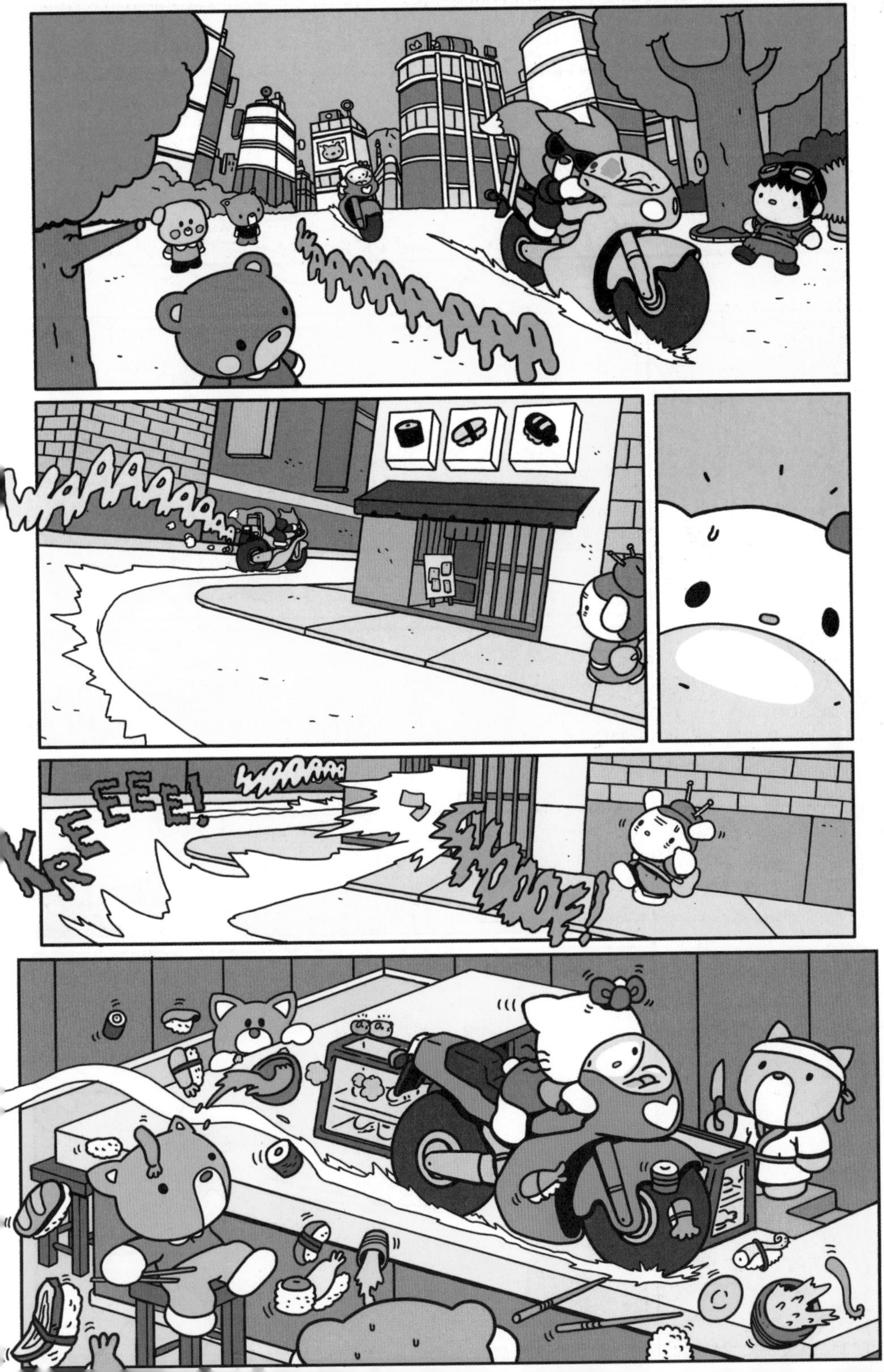
WAAAAAAAAAA
WAAAAAAAAAAAA
KREEEE!
WAAAAAA
SHOOOF!!

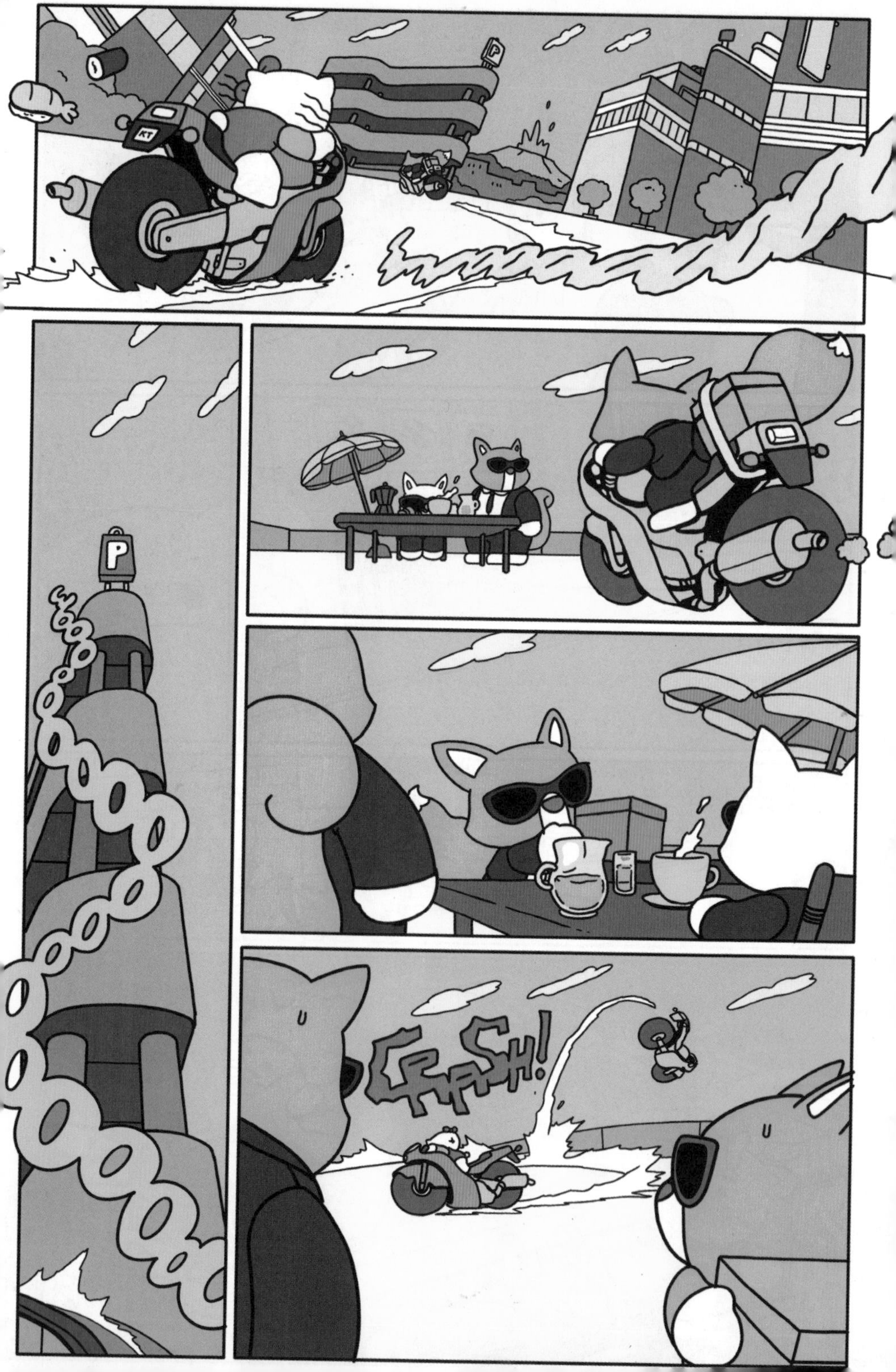
KT
P
P
CRASH!

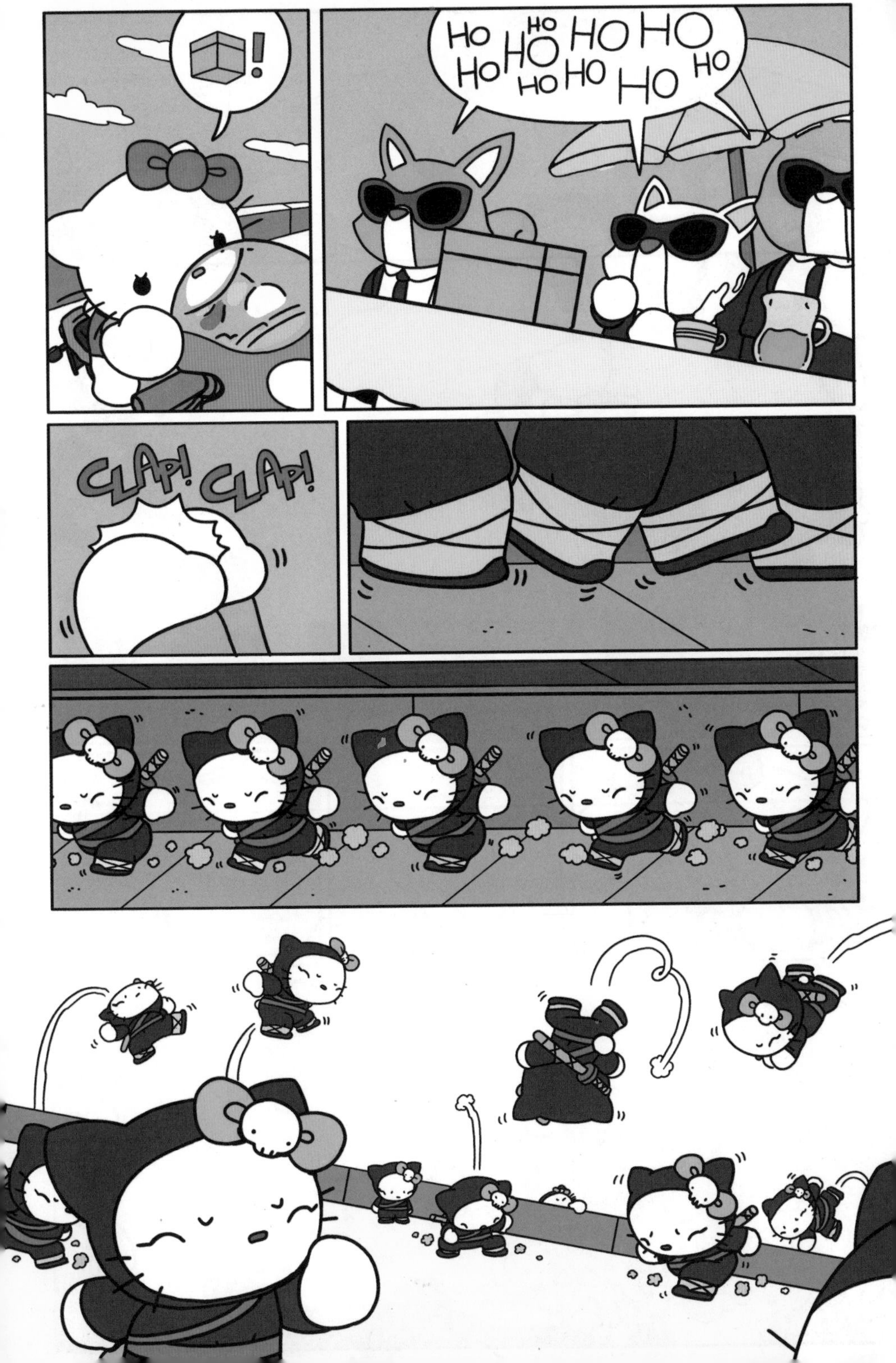
!
HO HO HO HO HO
HO HO HO HO HO HO HO
CLAP! CLAP!

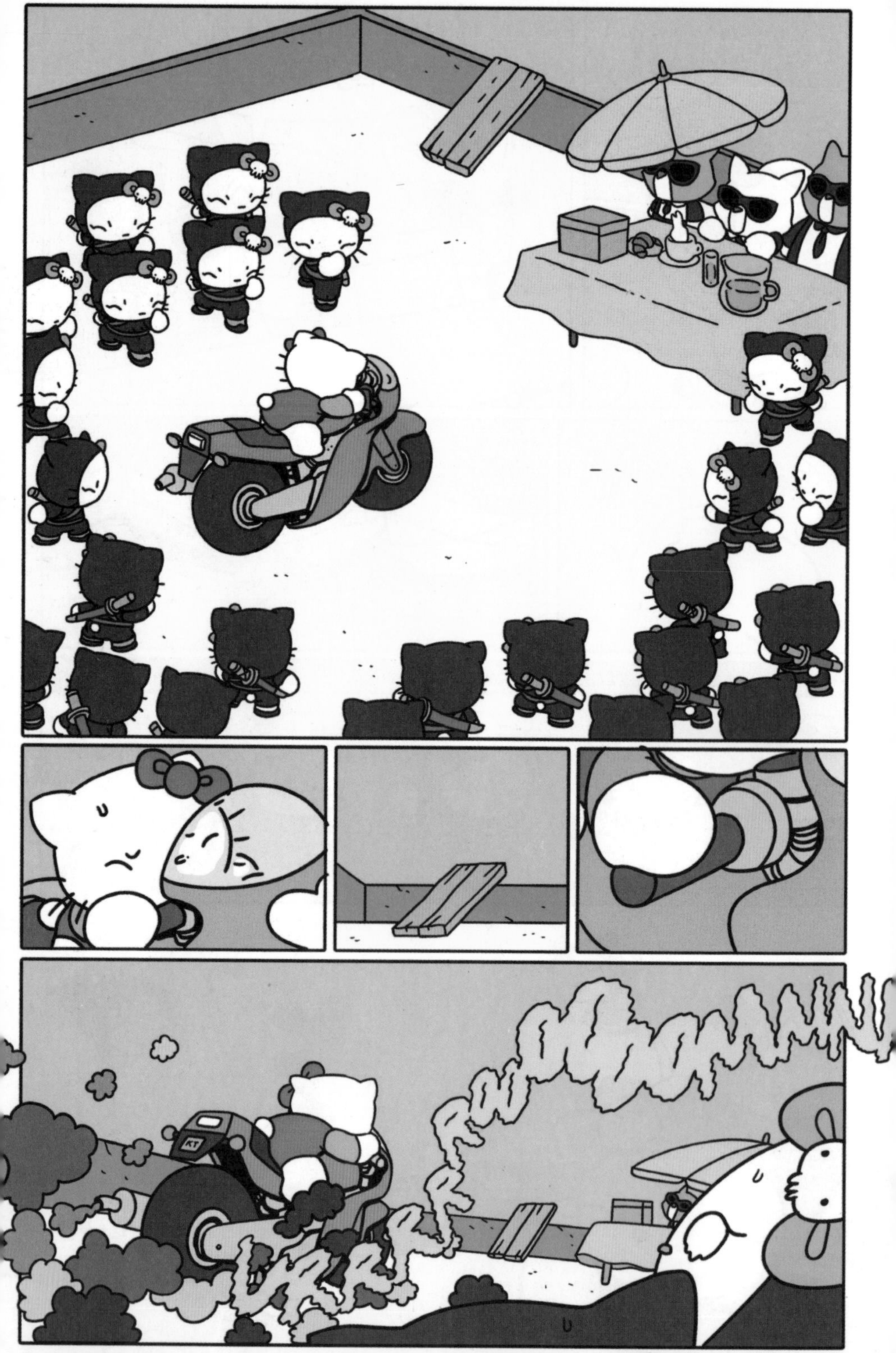

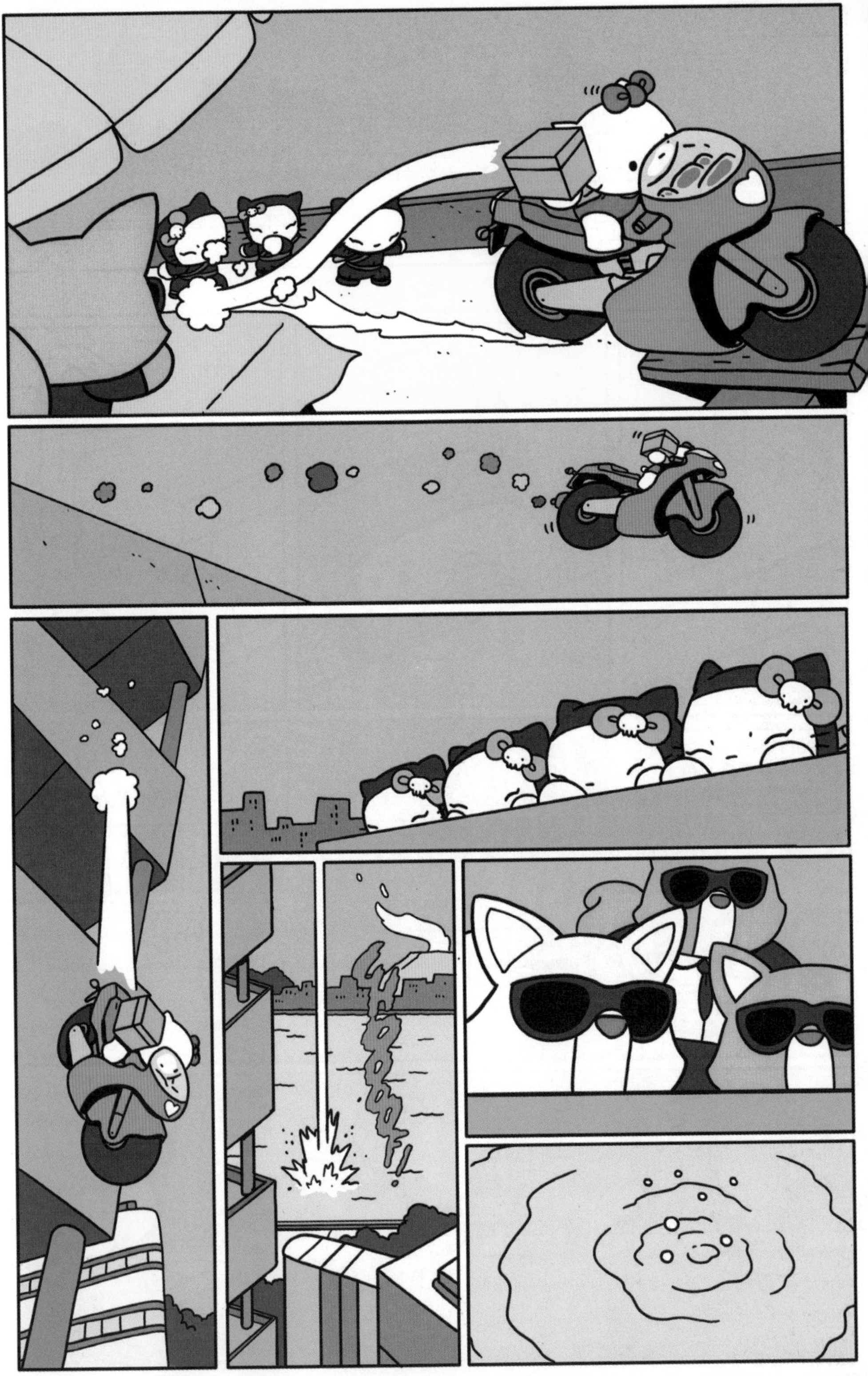

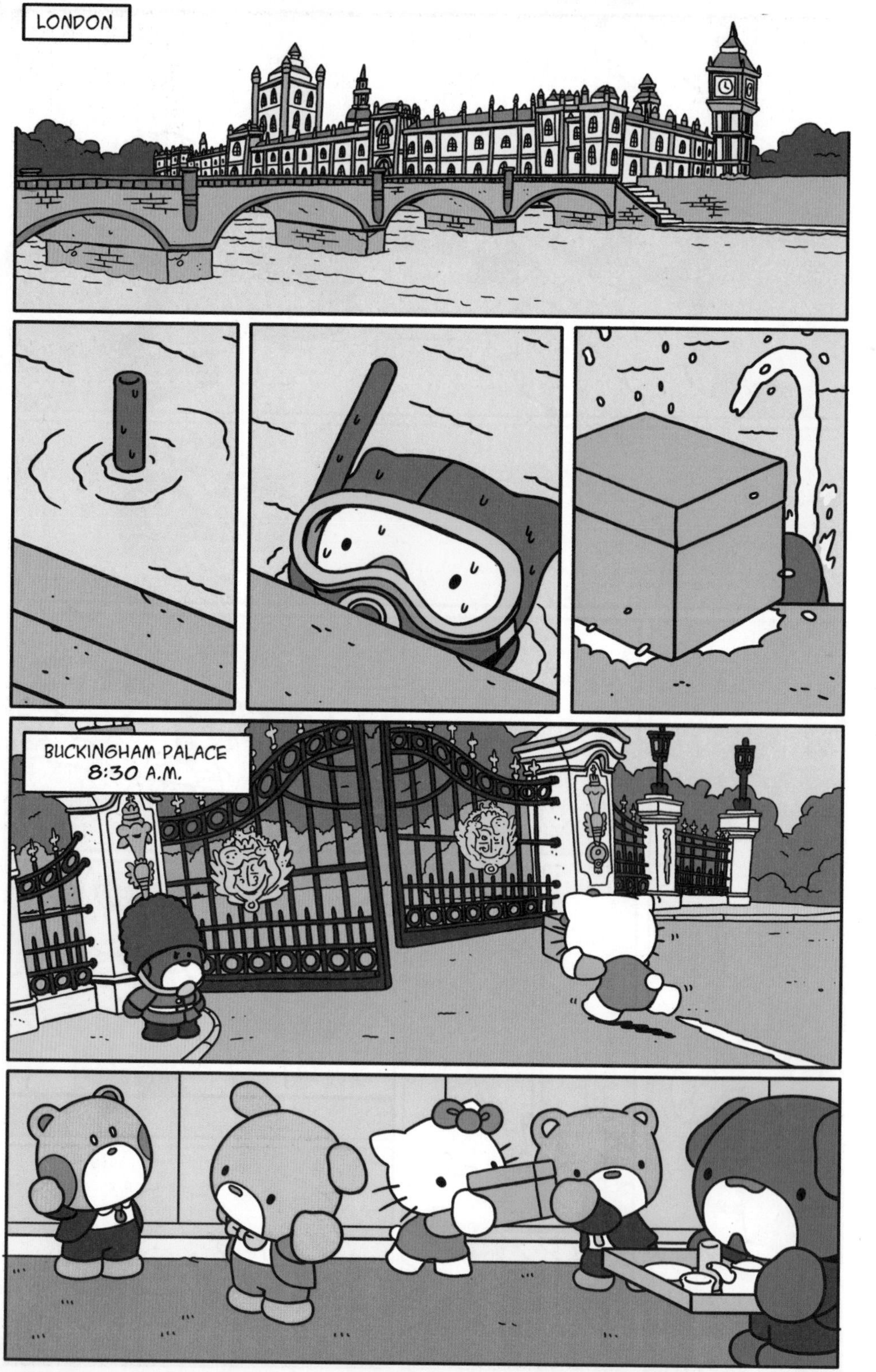
LONDON
BUCKINGHAM PALACE
8:30 A.M.

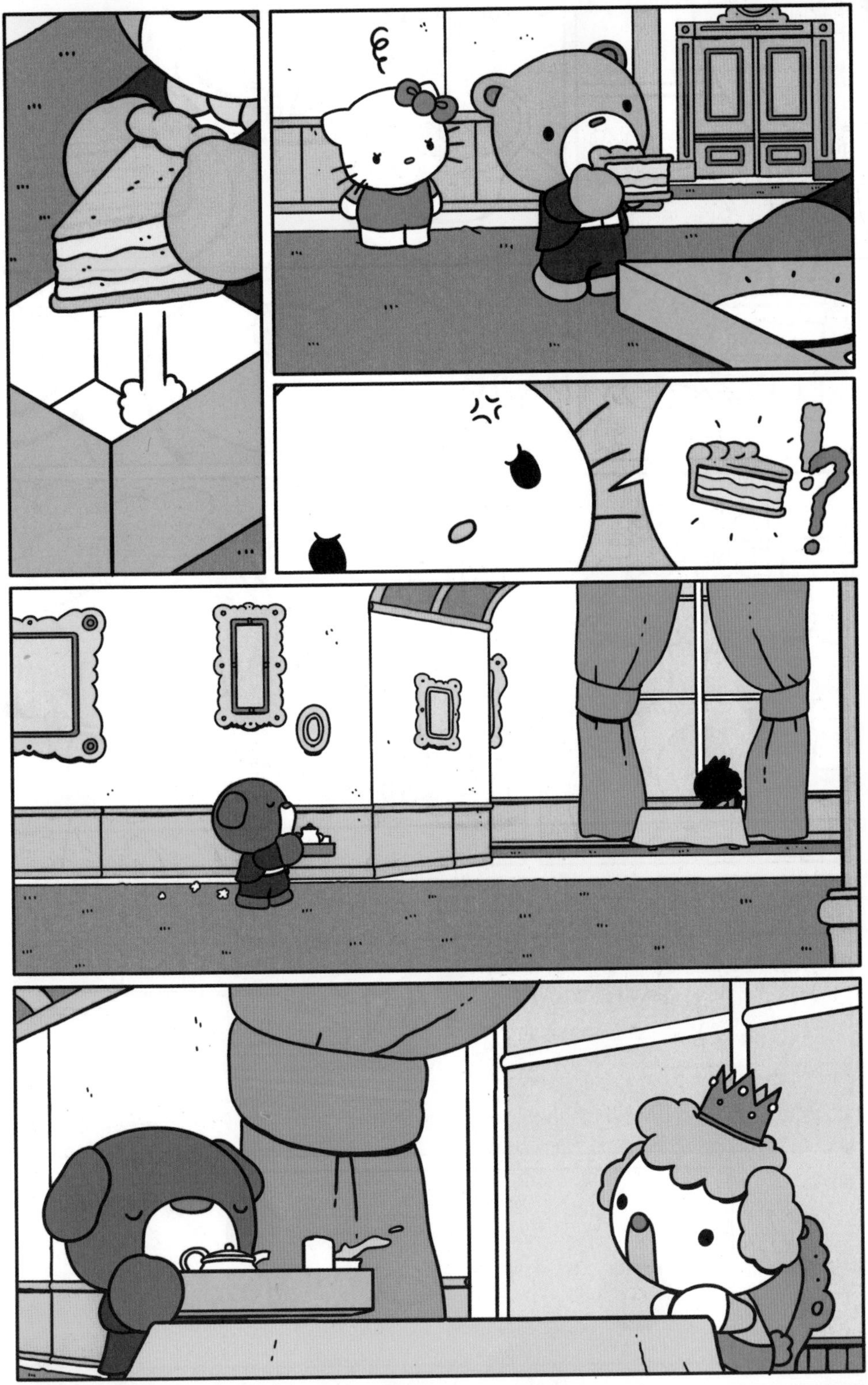

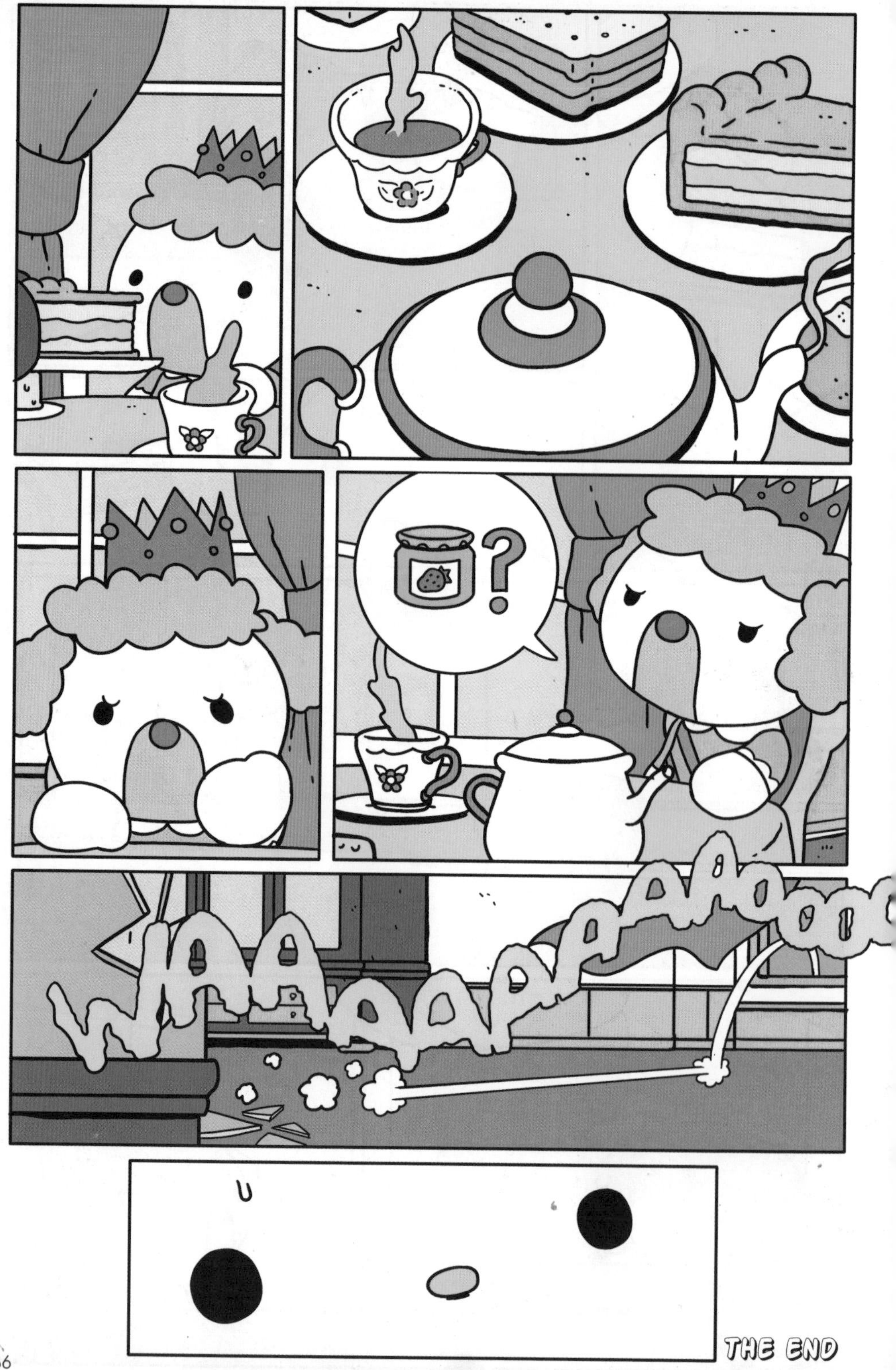
?
WHAAAAAAAAOOOO
THE END

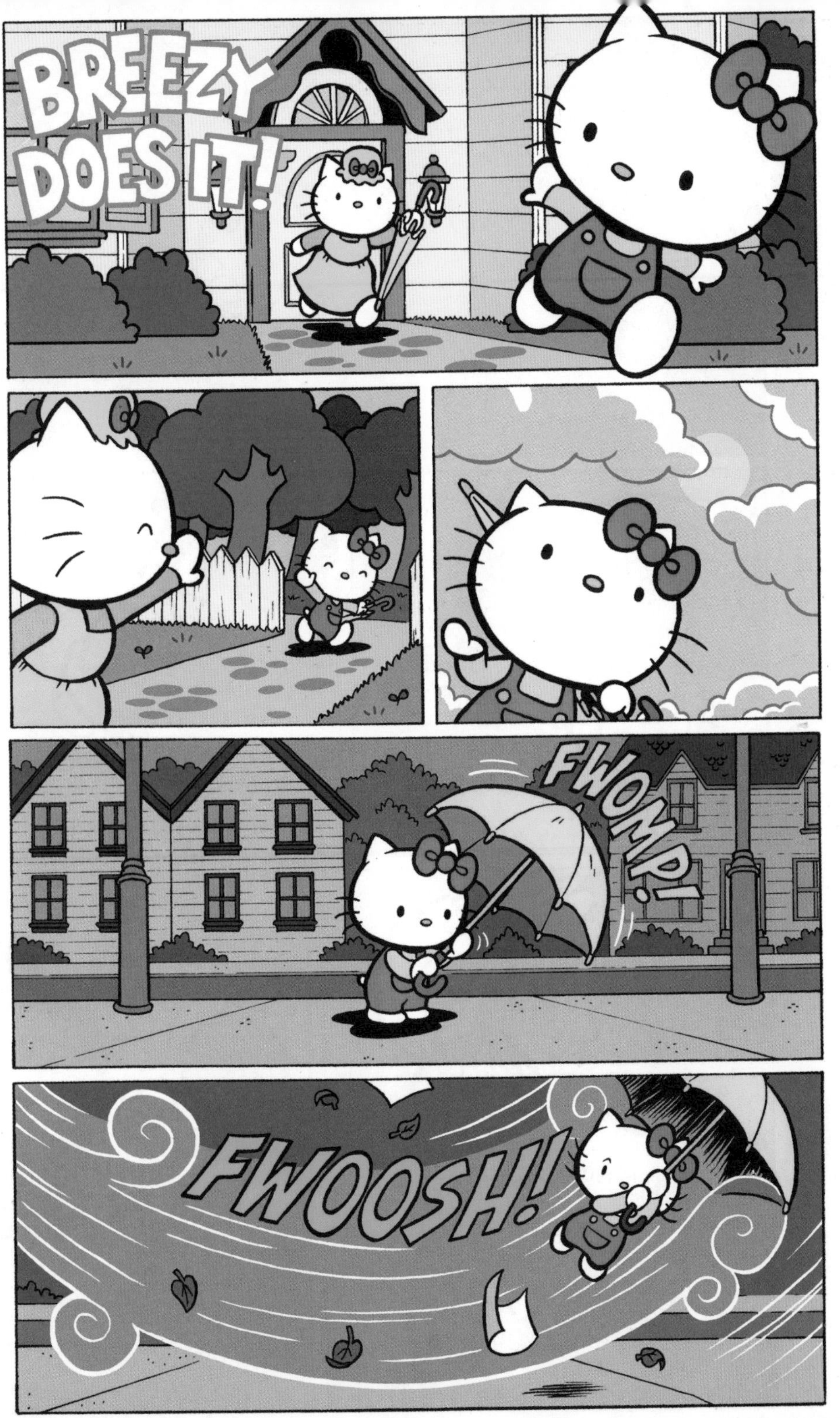
BREEZY DOES IT!
FWOMP!
FWOOSH!

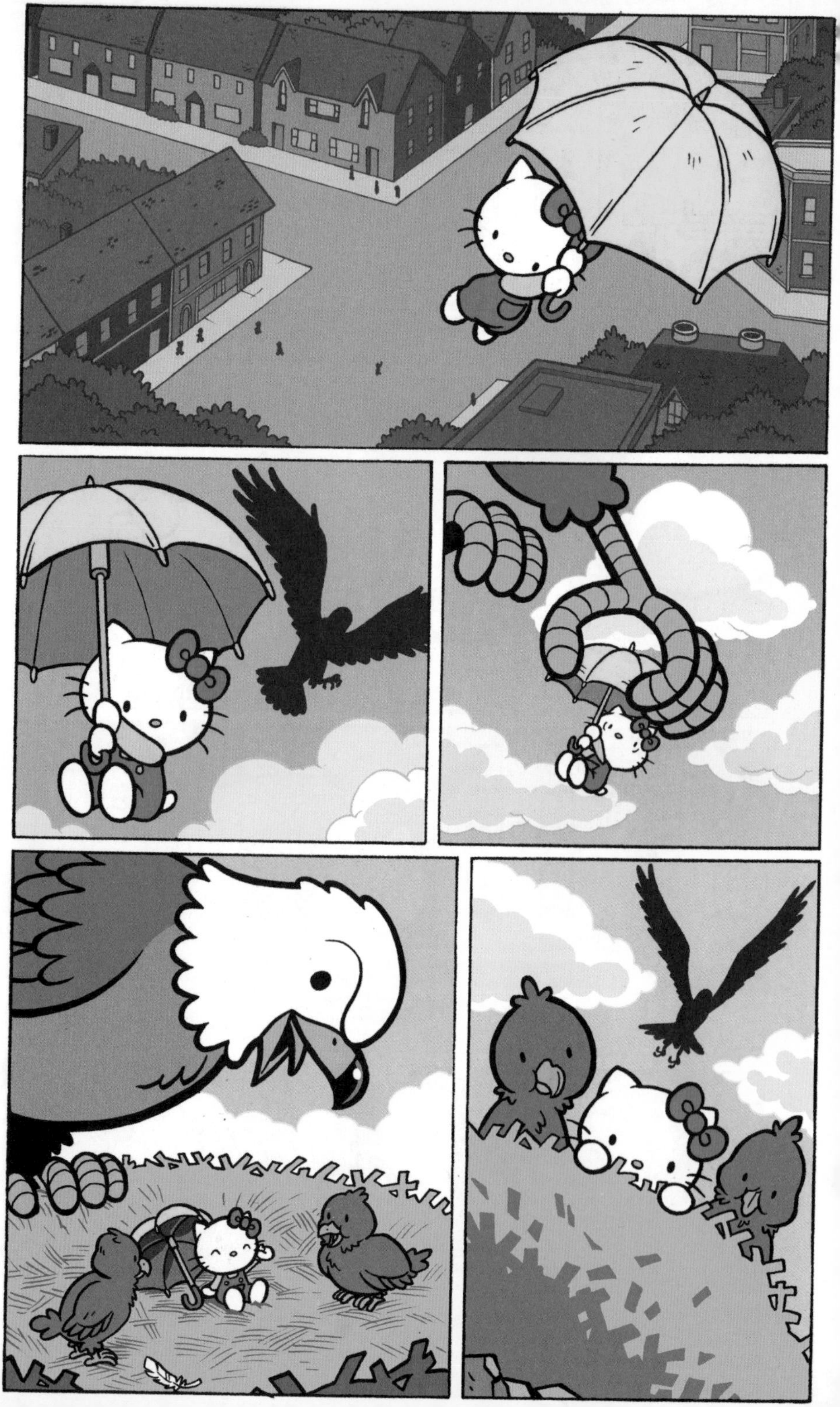

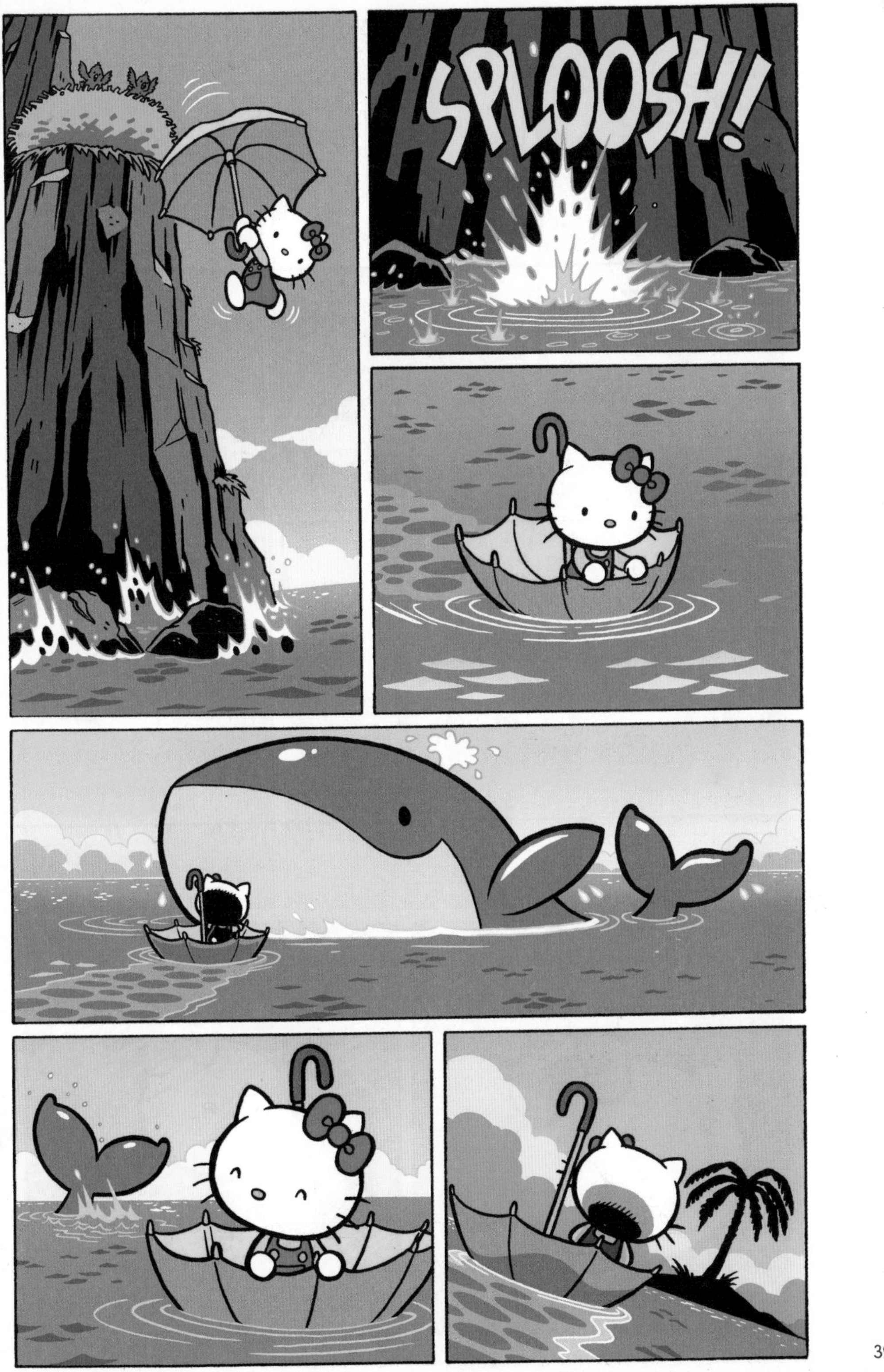
SPLOOSH!

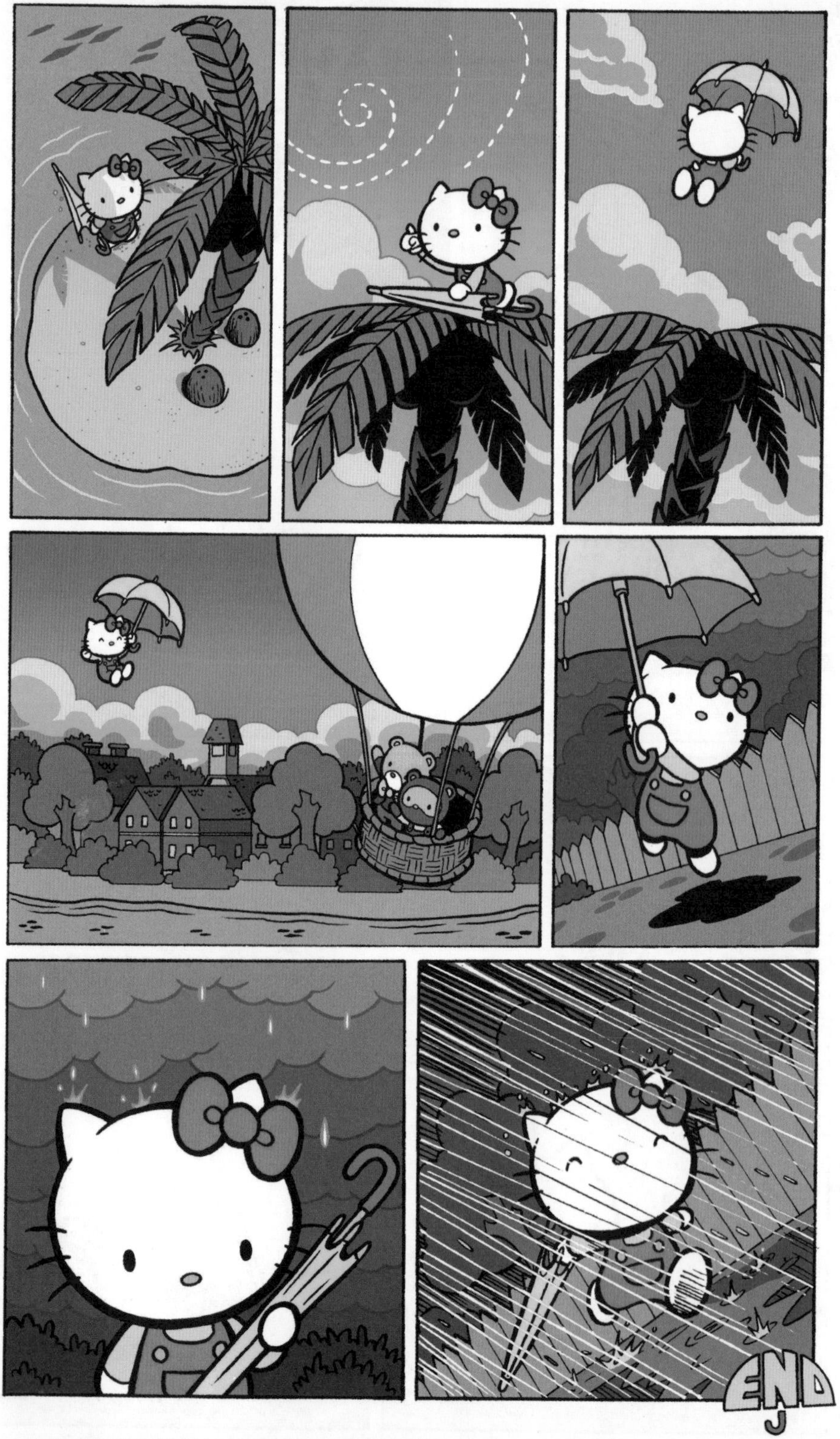
END

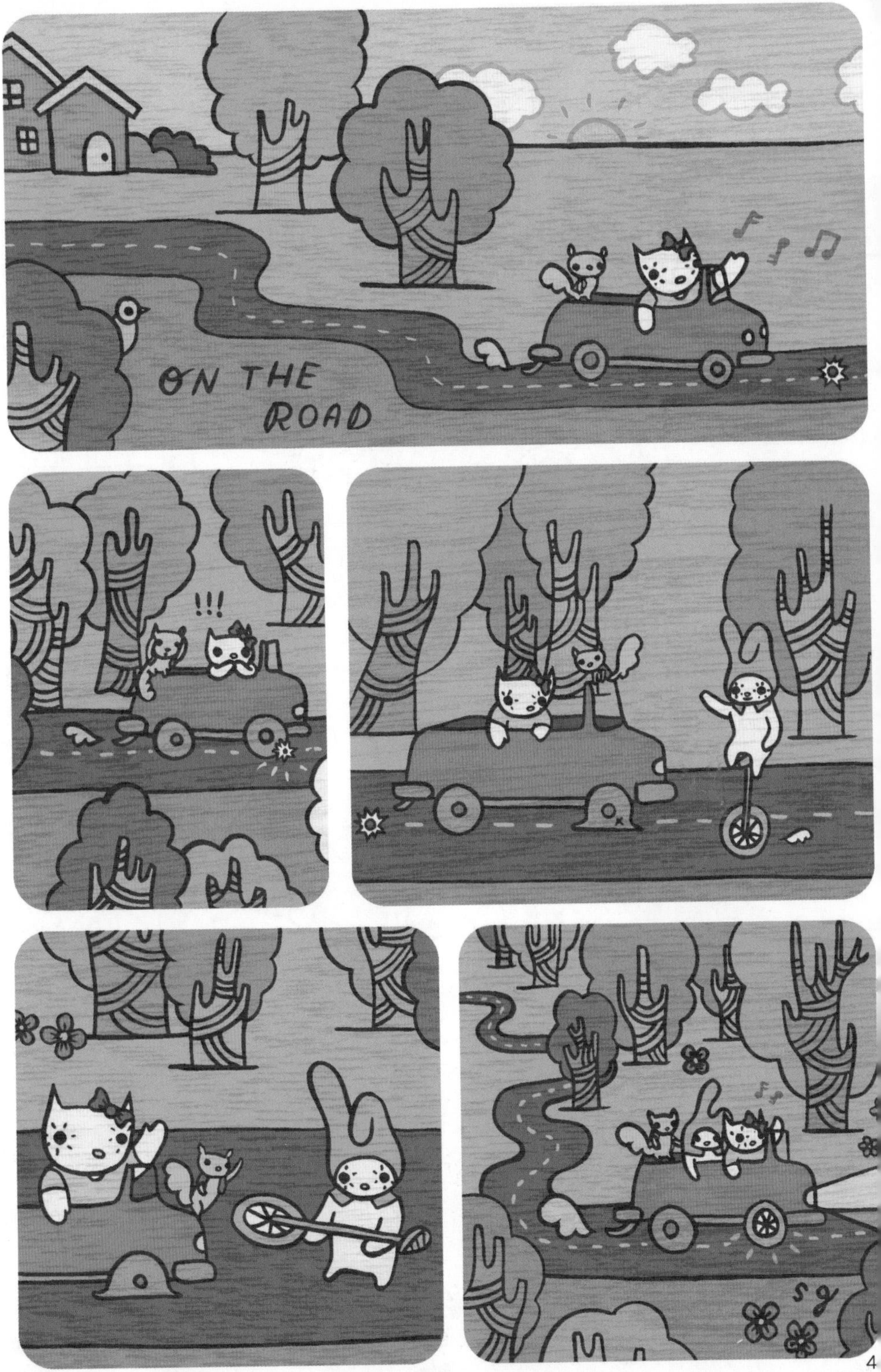
ON THE ROAD
!!!
sg

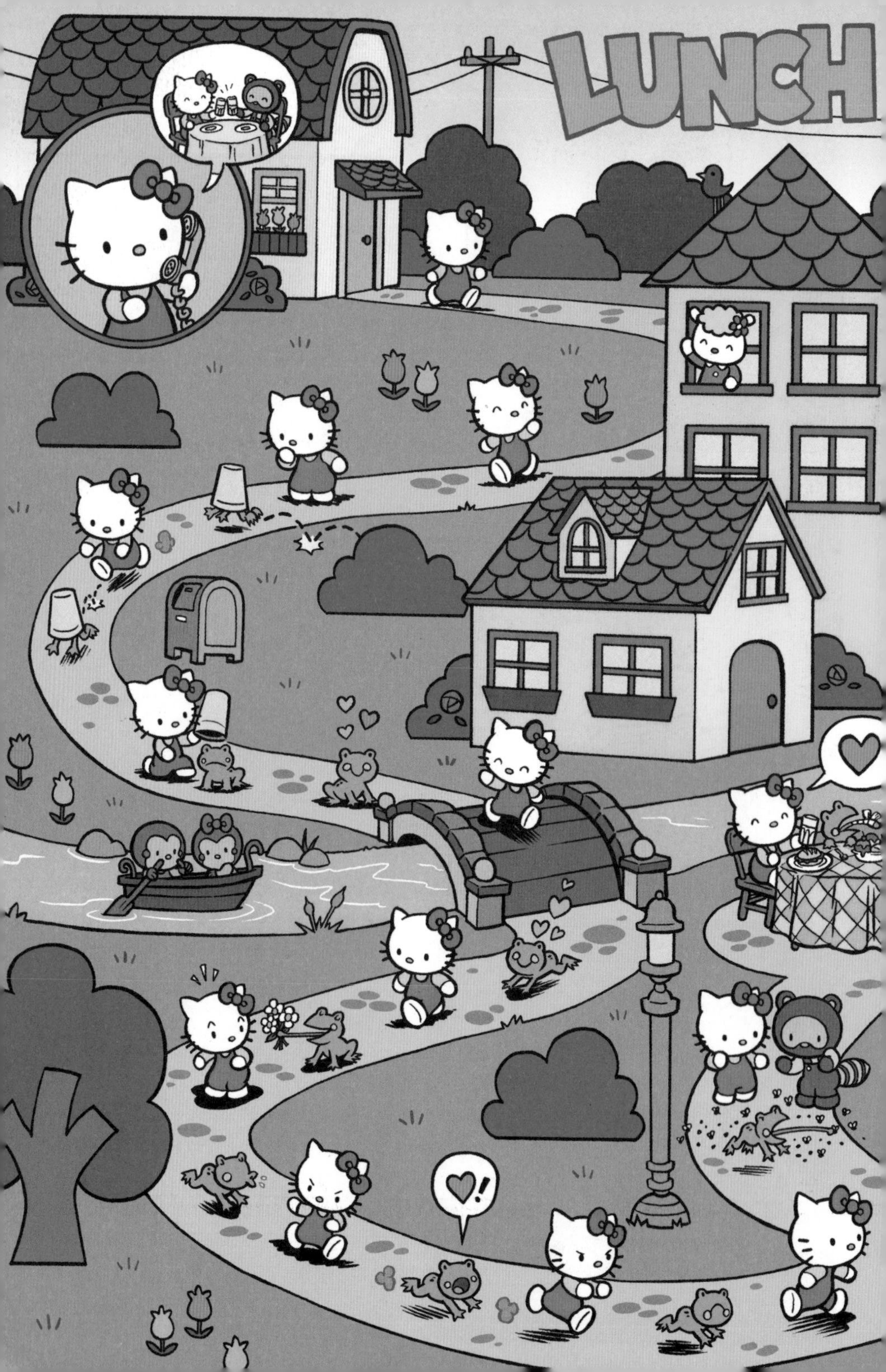
LUNCH

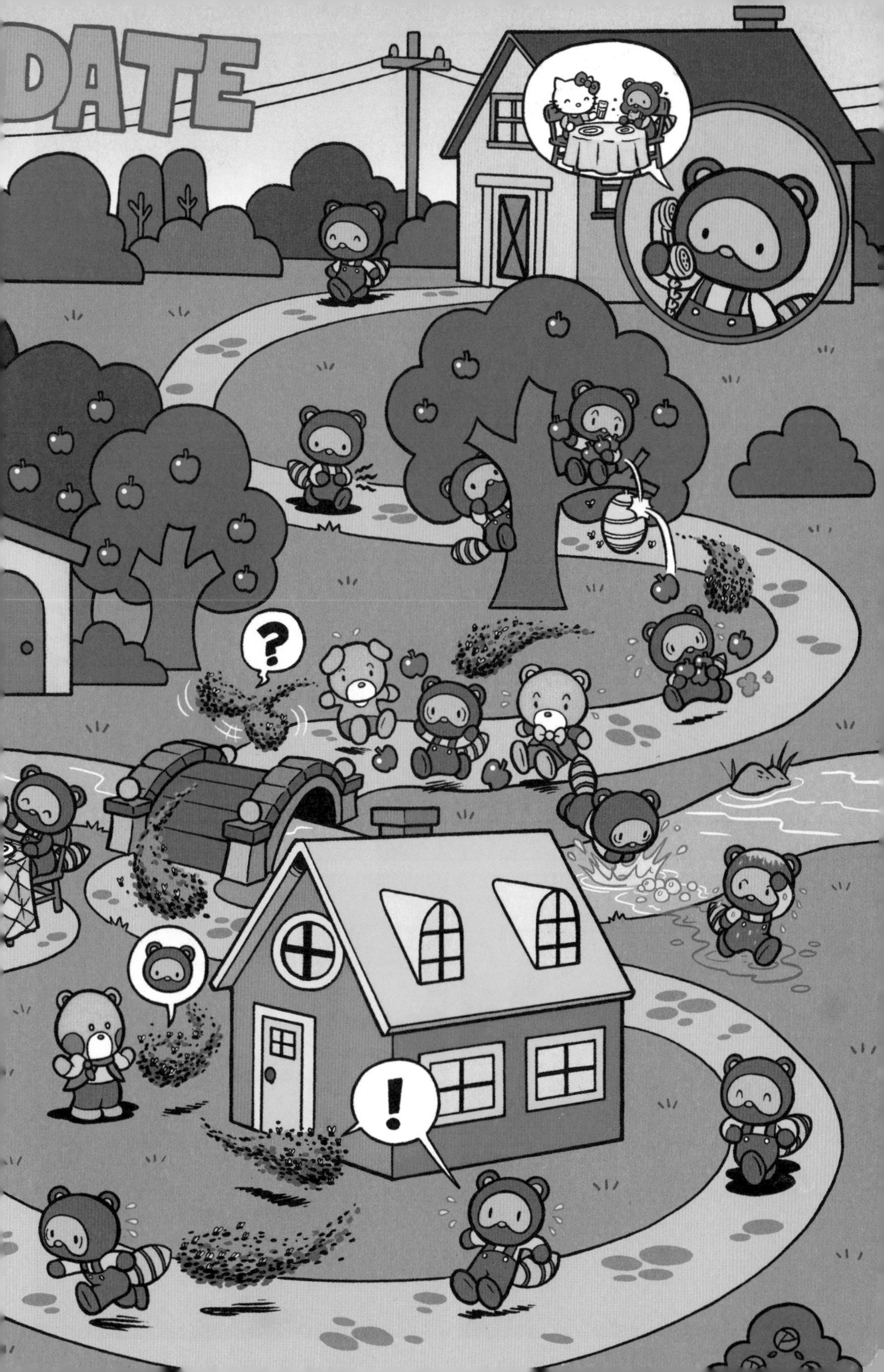
DATE
?
!

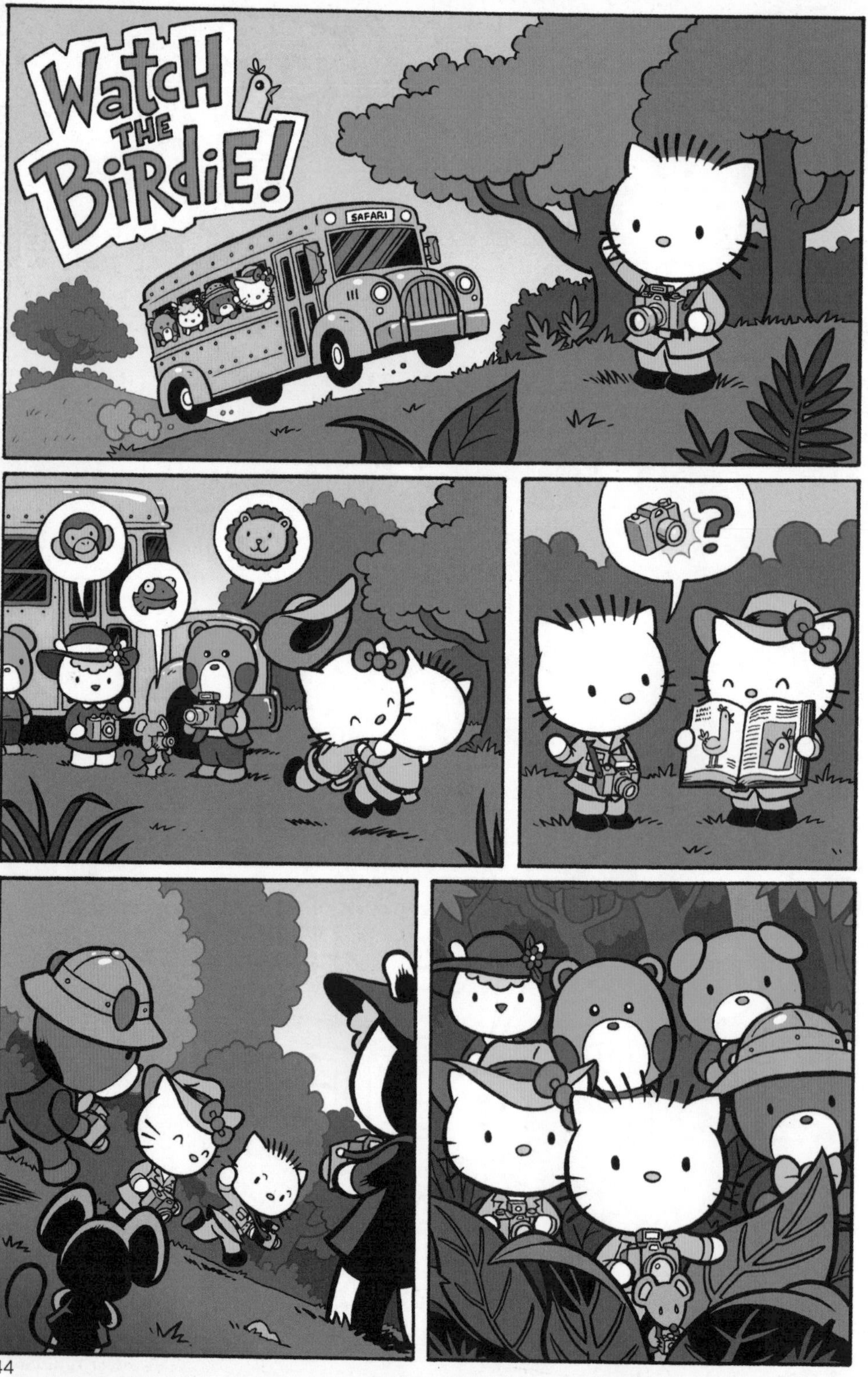
Watch THE BirdiE!
SAFARI
?

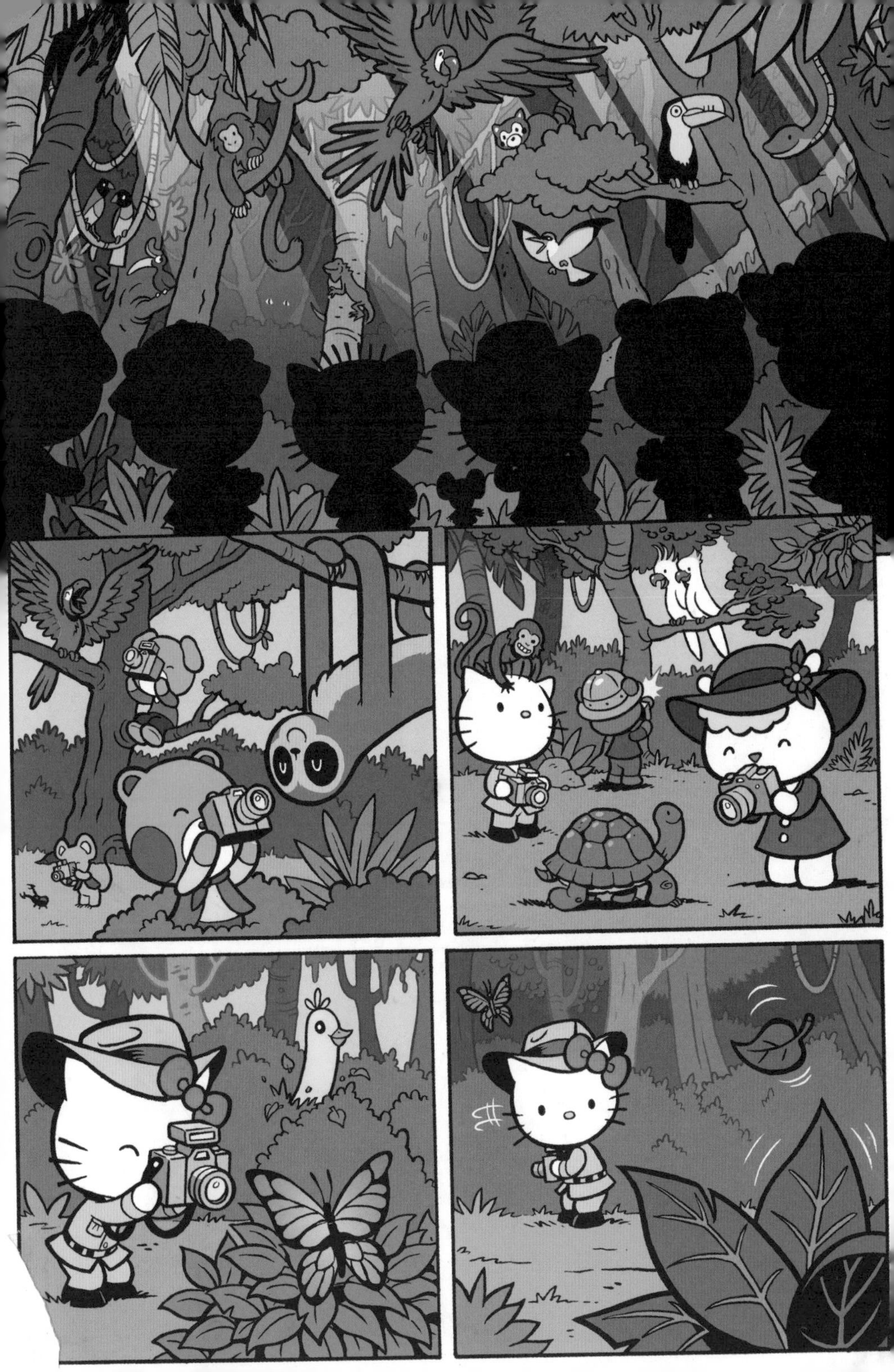

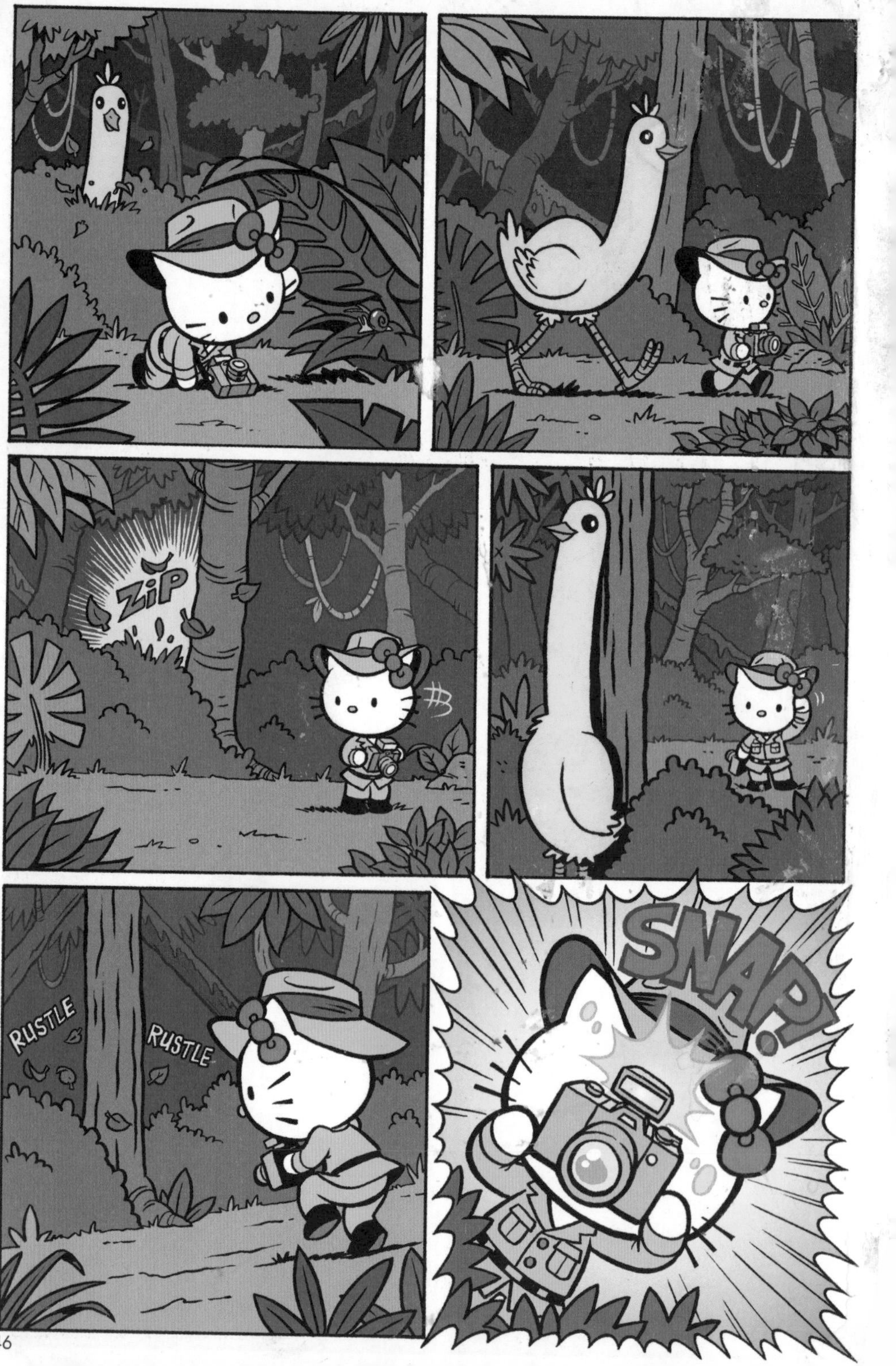
ZIP
RUSTLE
RUSTLE
SNAP!

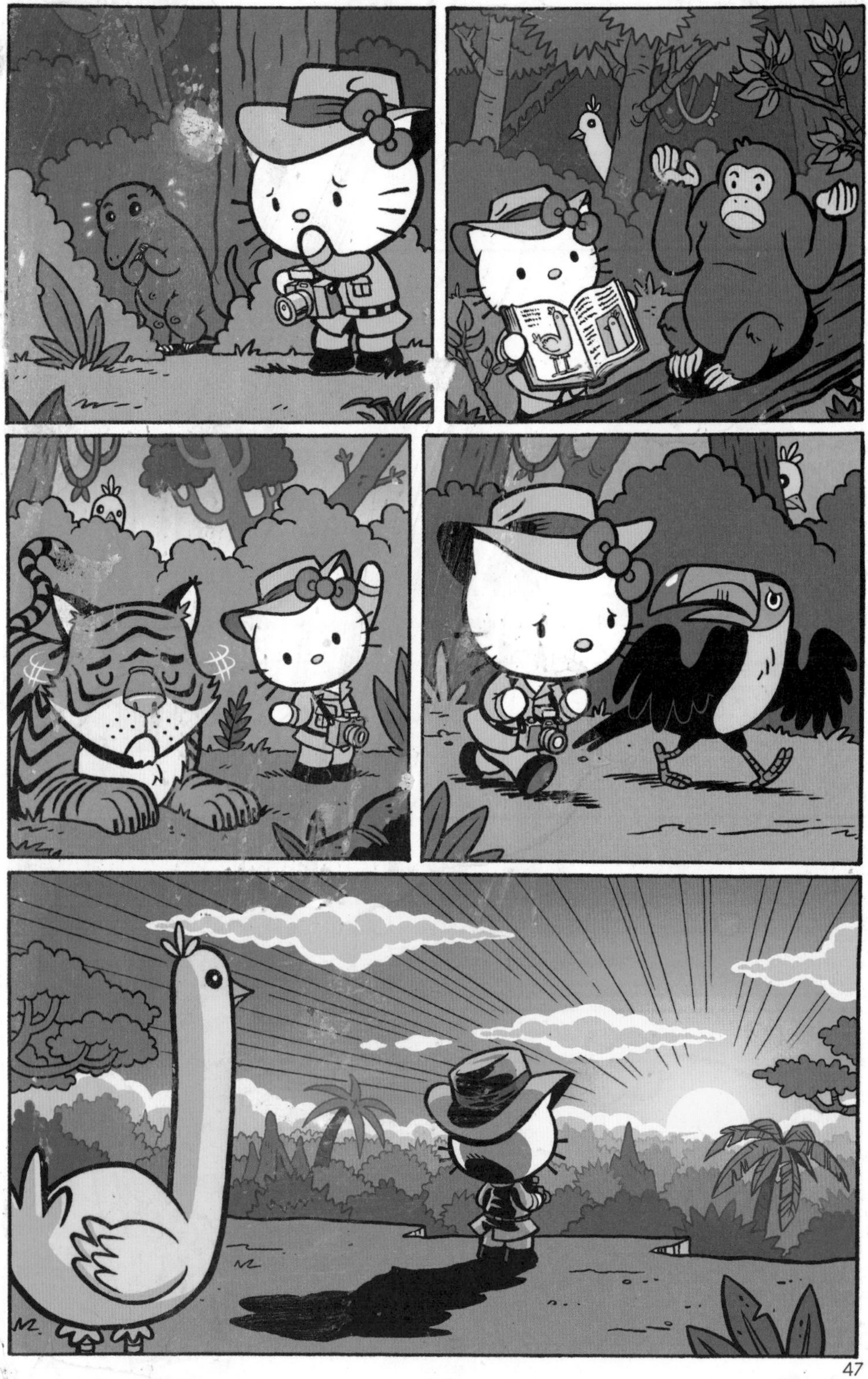

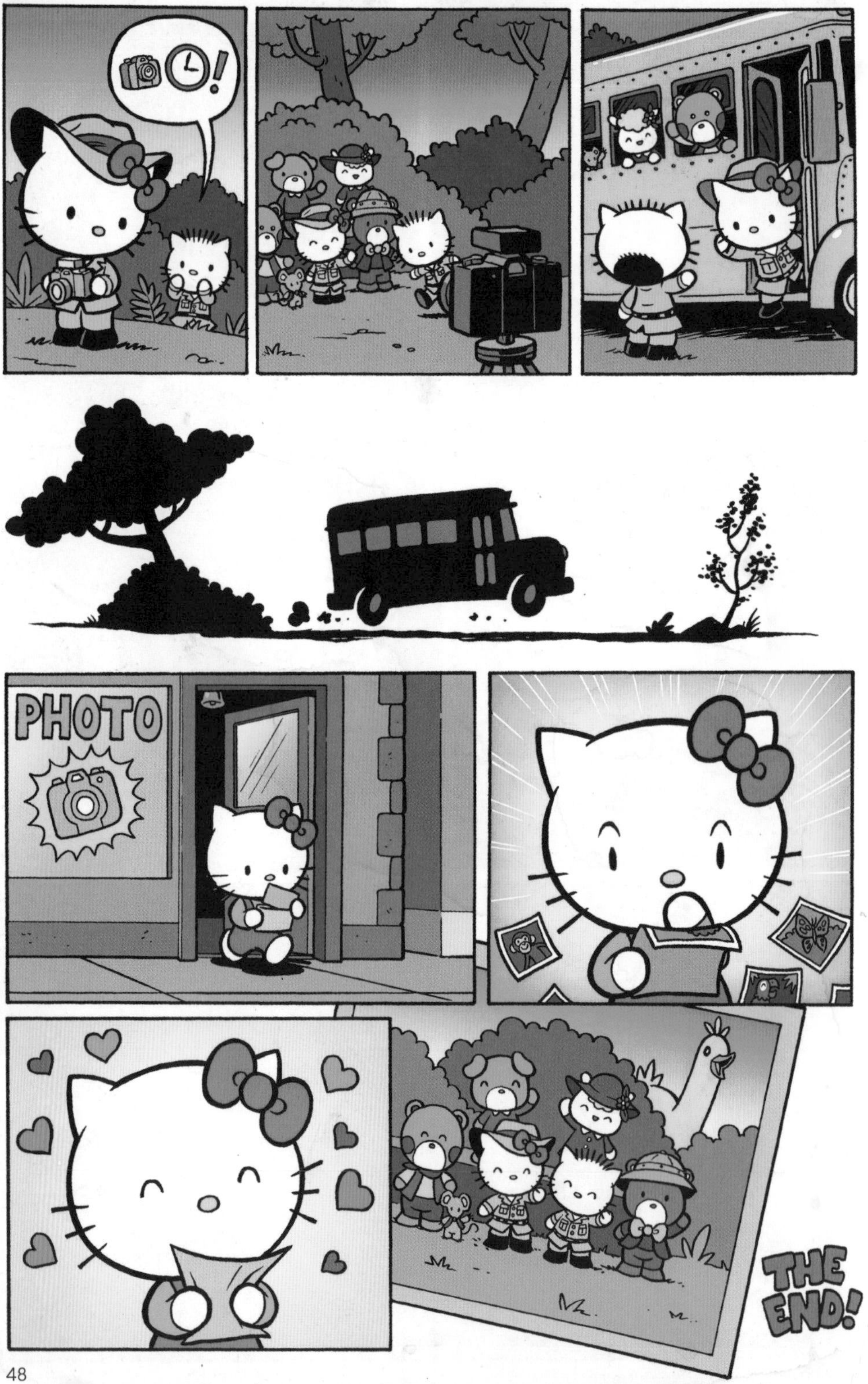
!
PHOTO
THE END!

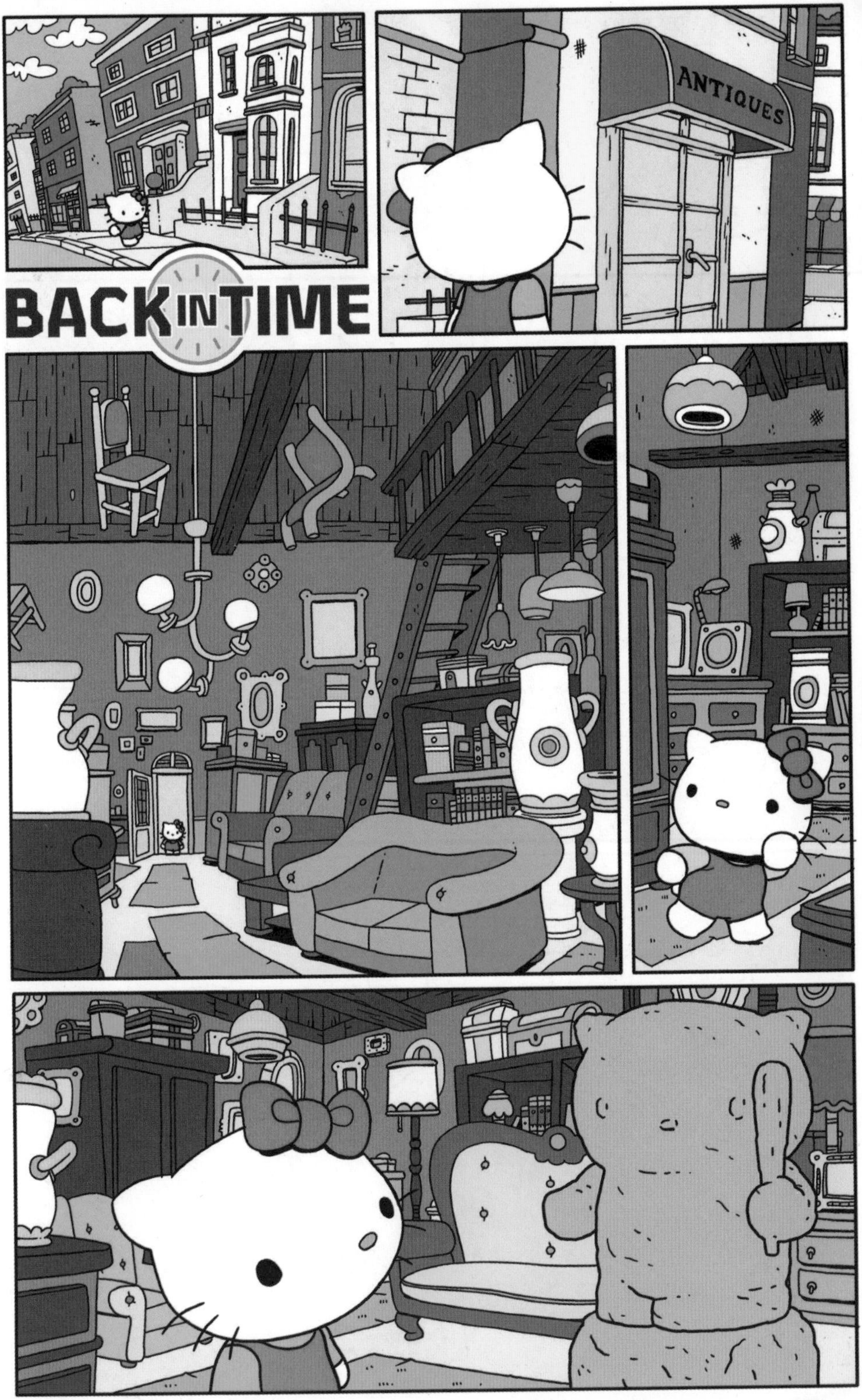
BACK IN TIME
ANTIQUES

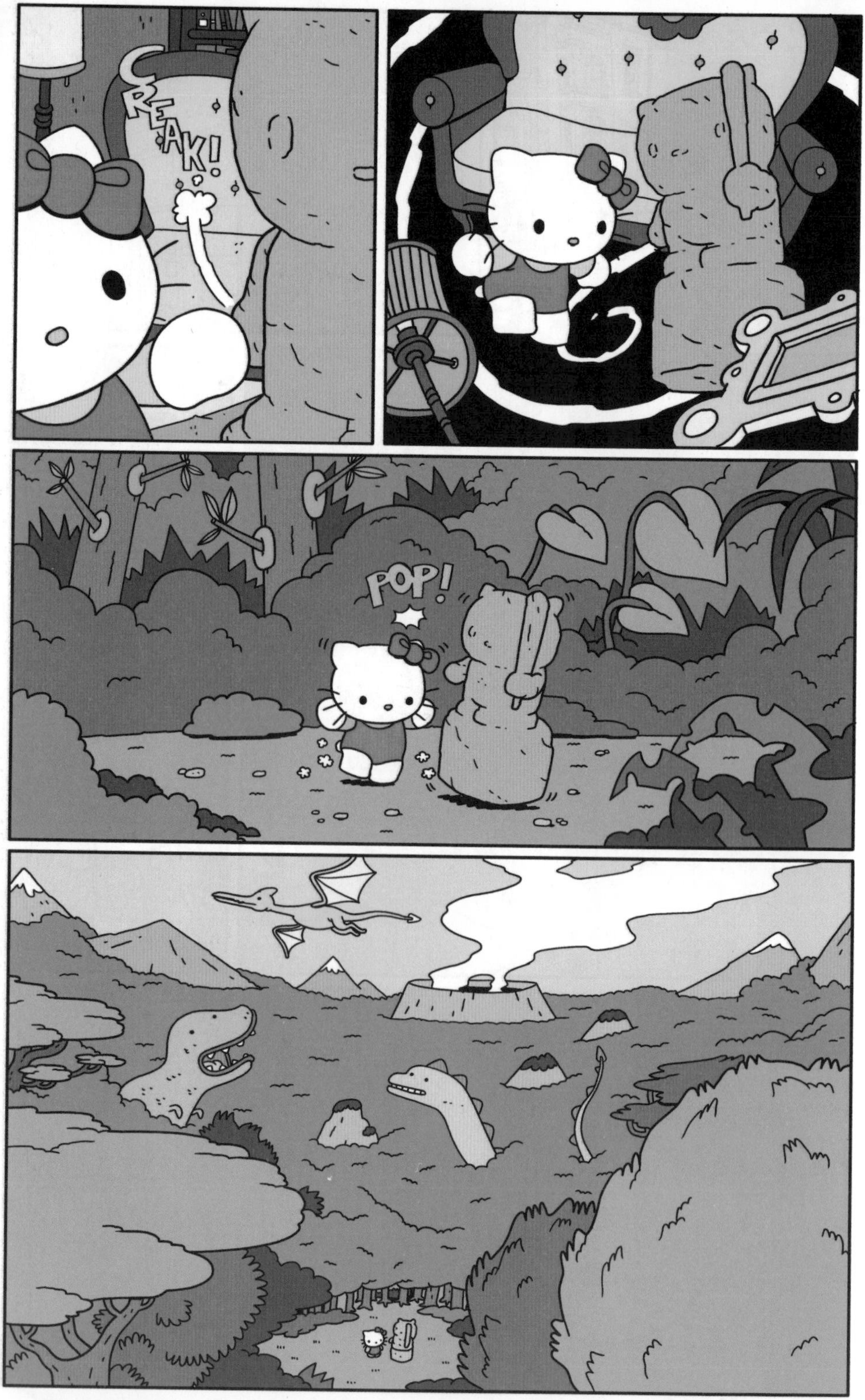
CREAK!
POP!

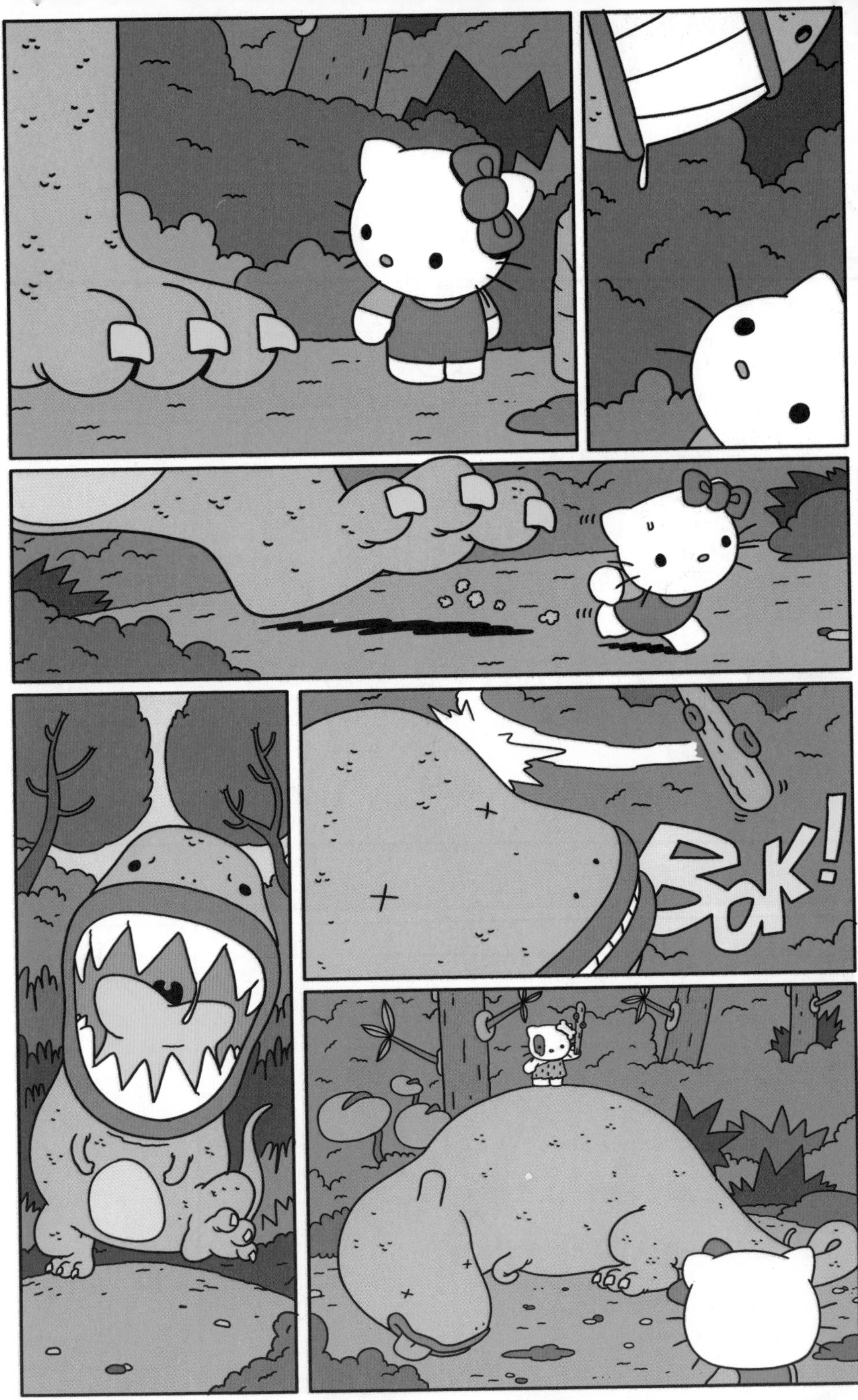
BOK!

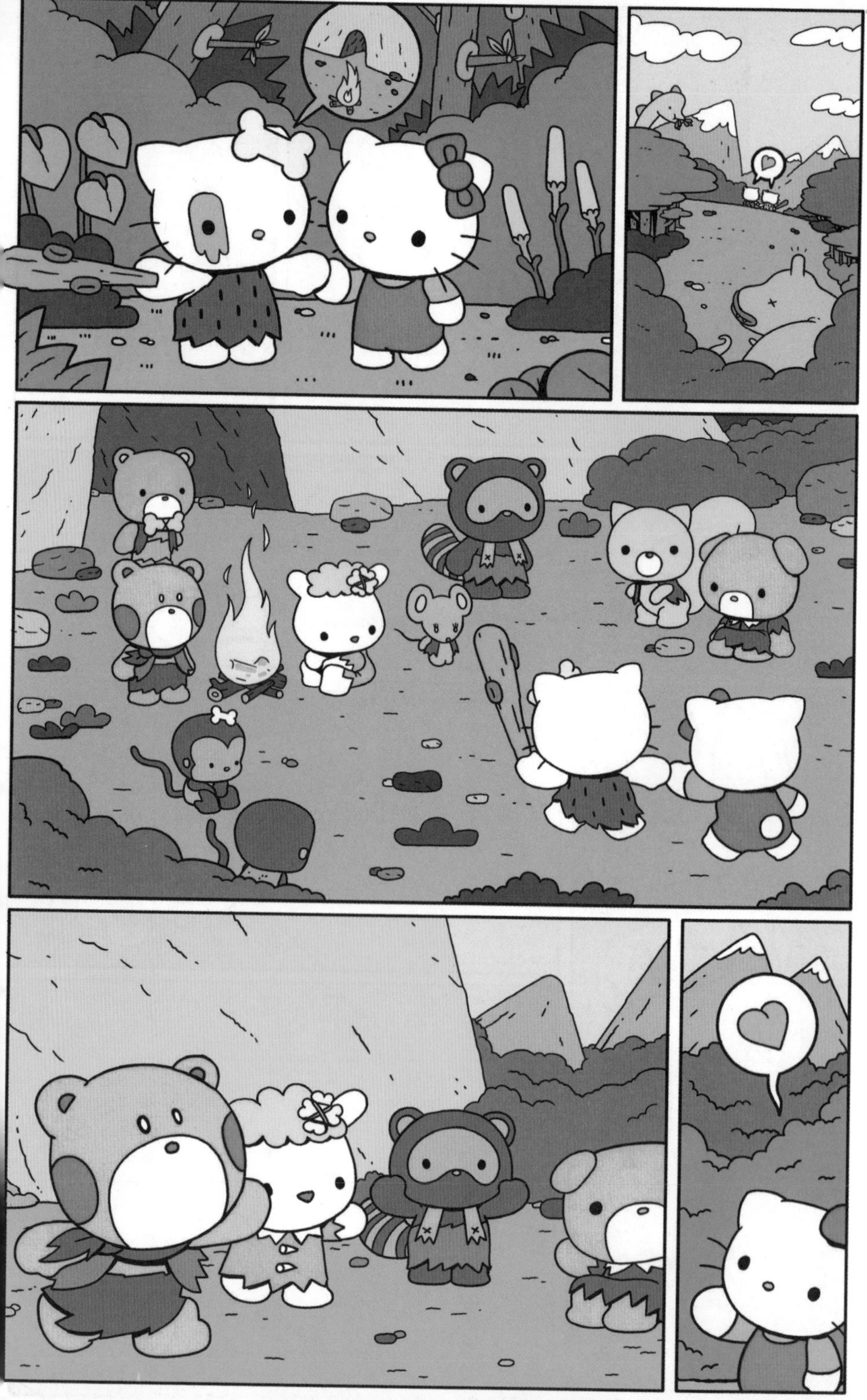

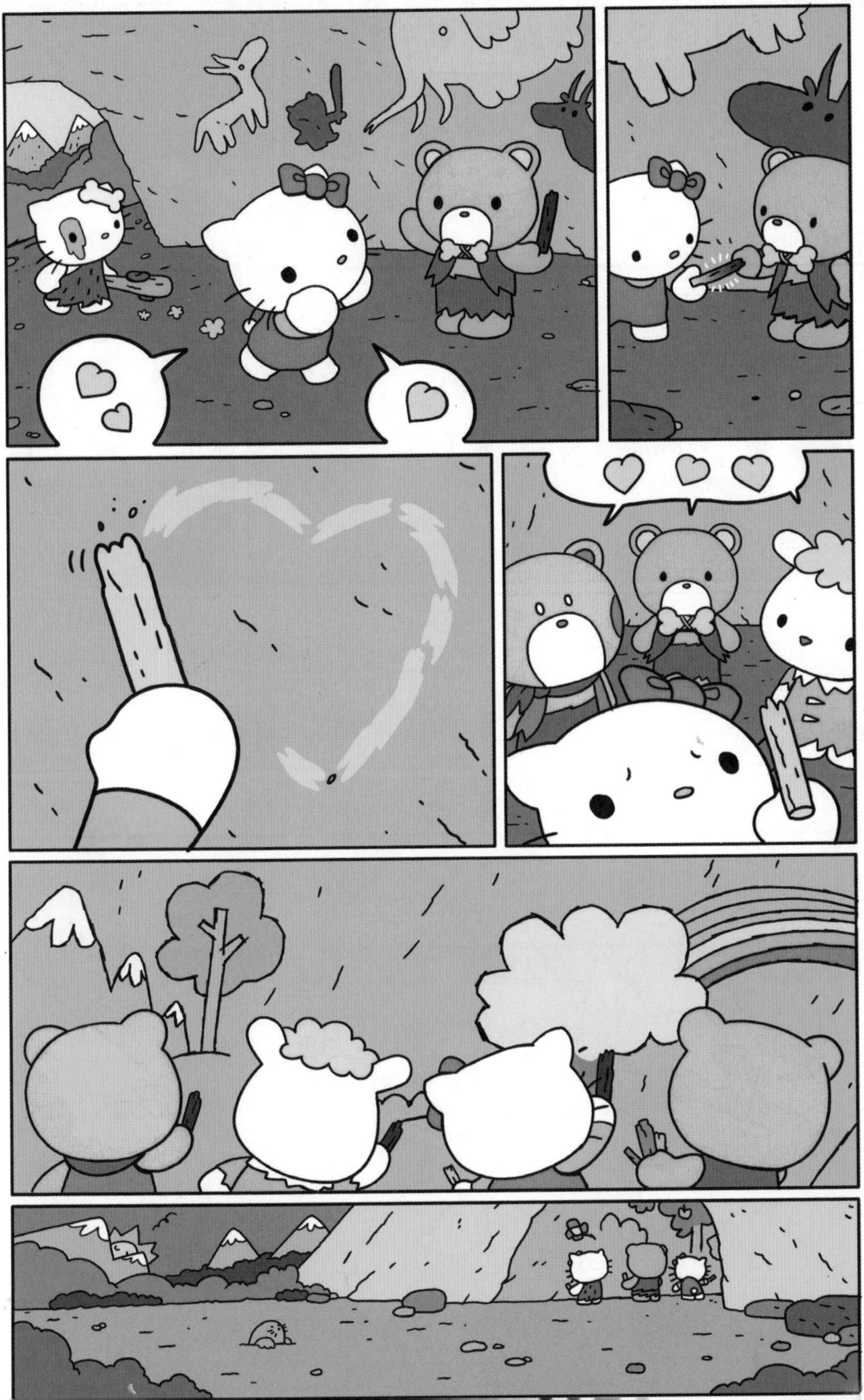

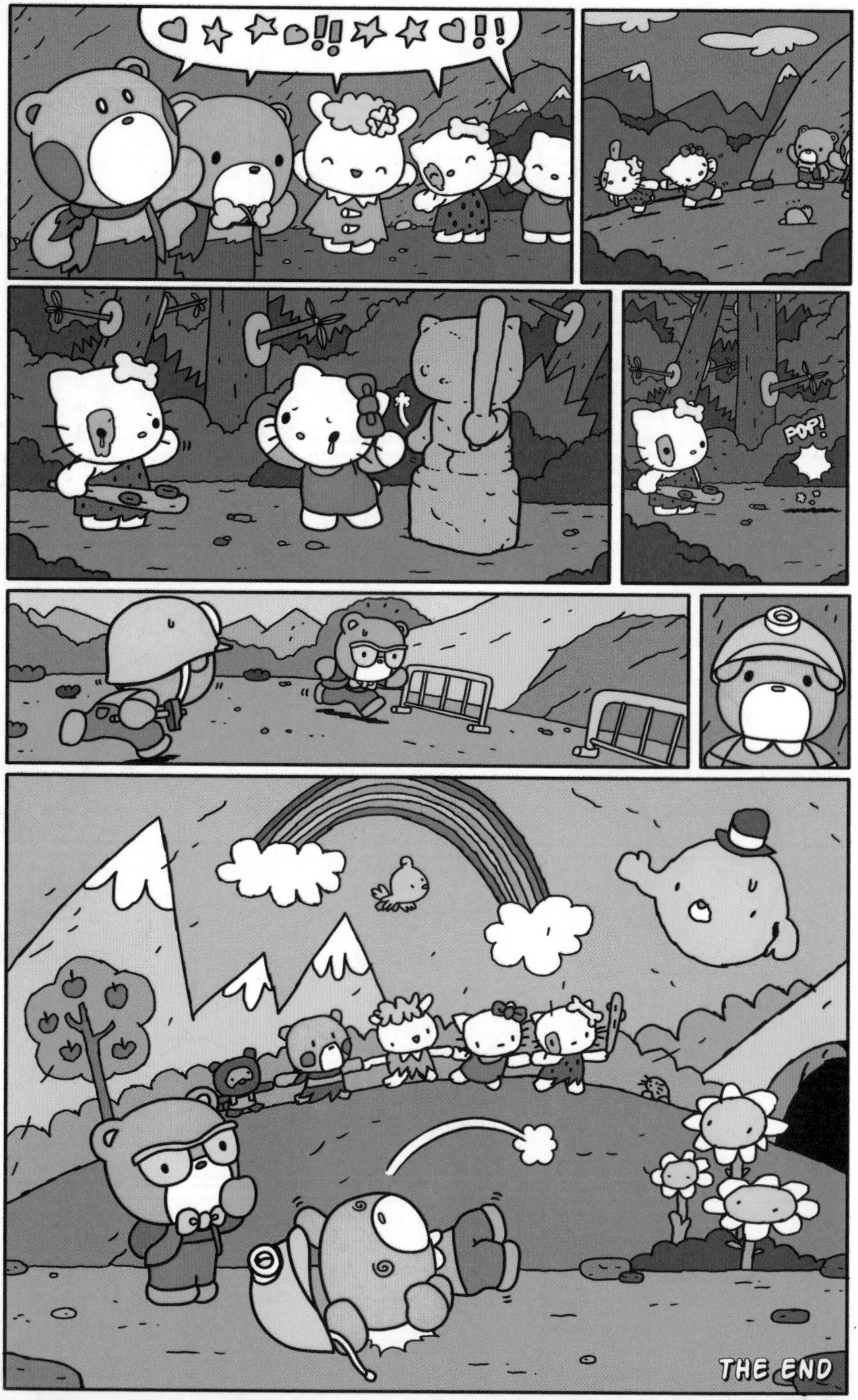
♡☆☆♡!!☆☆♡!!
POP!
THE END

TURN THE PAGE

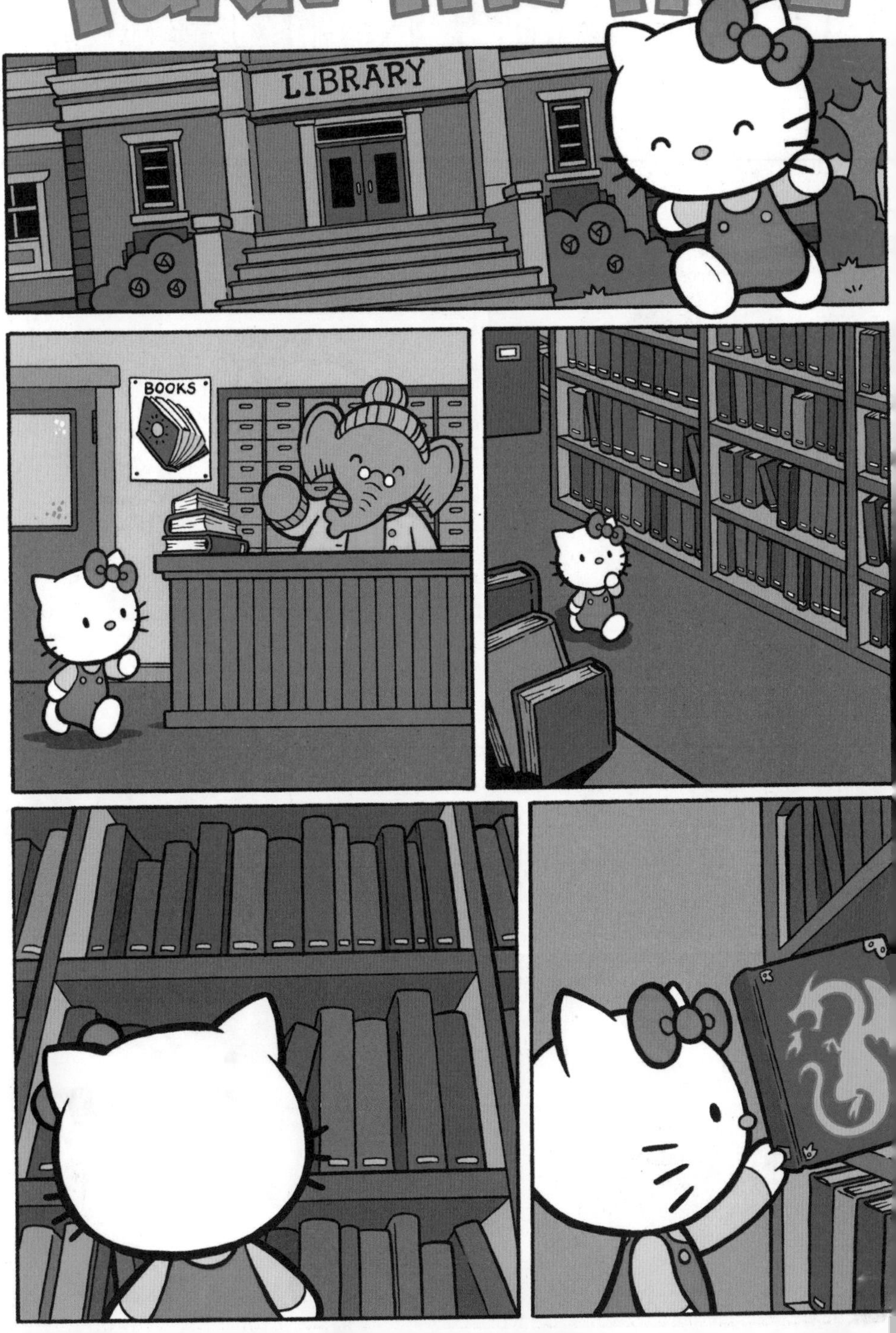
LIBRARY
BOOKS

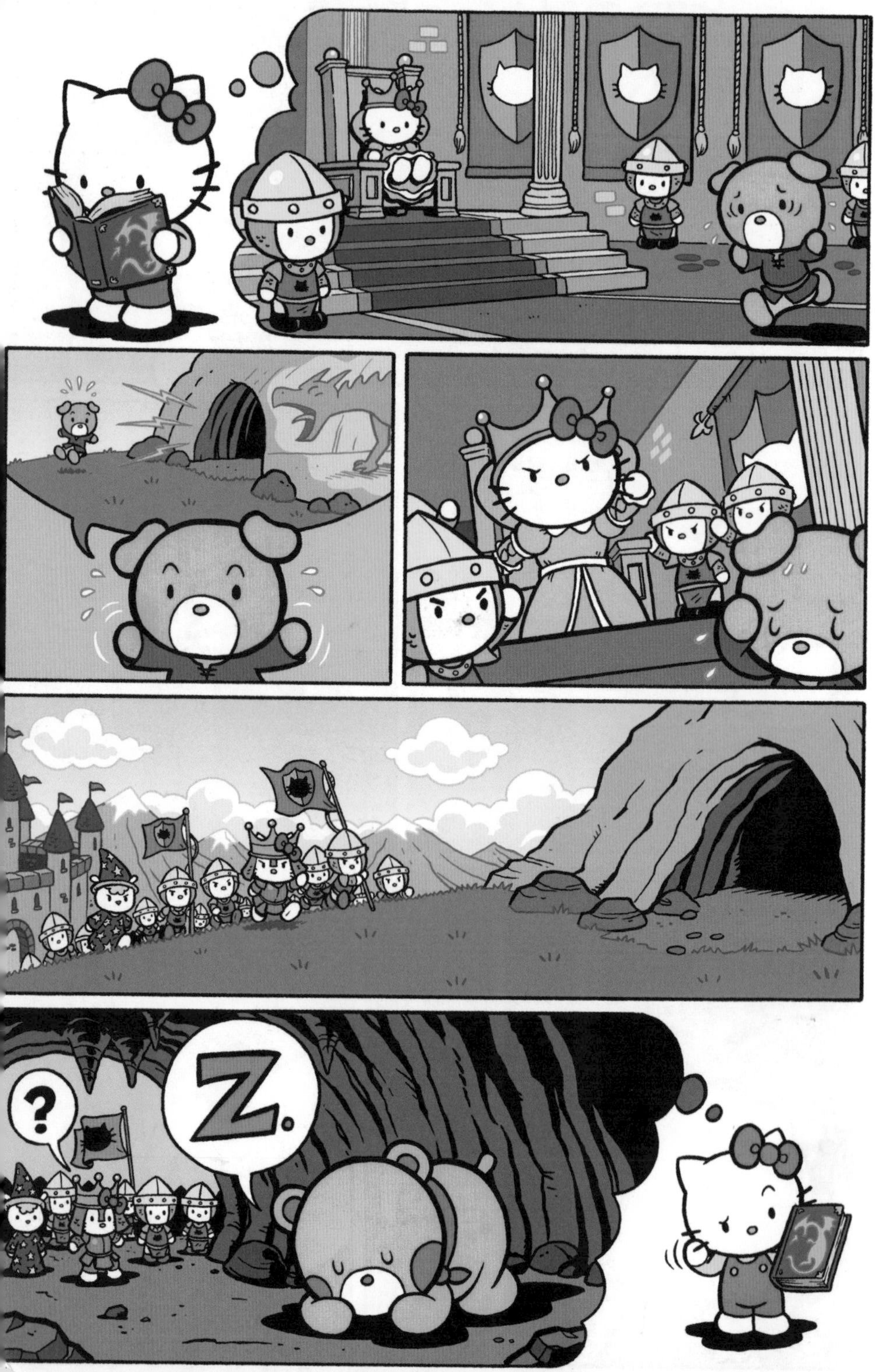
?
Z.

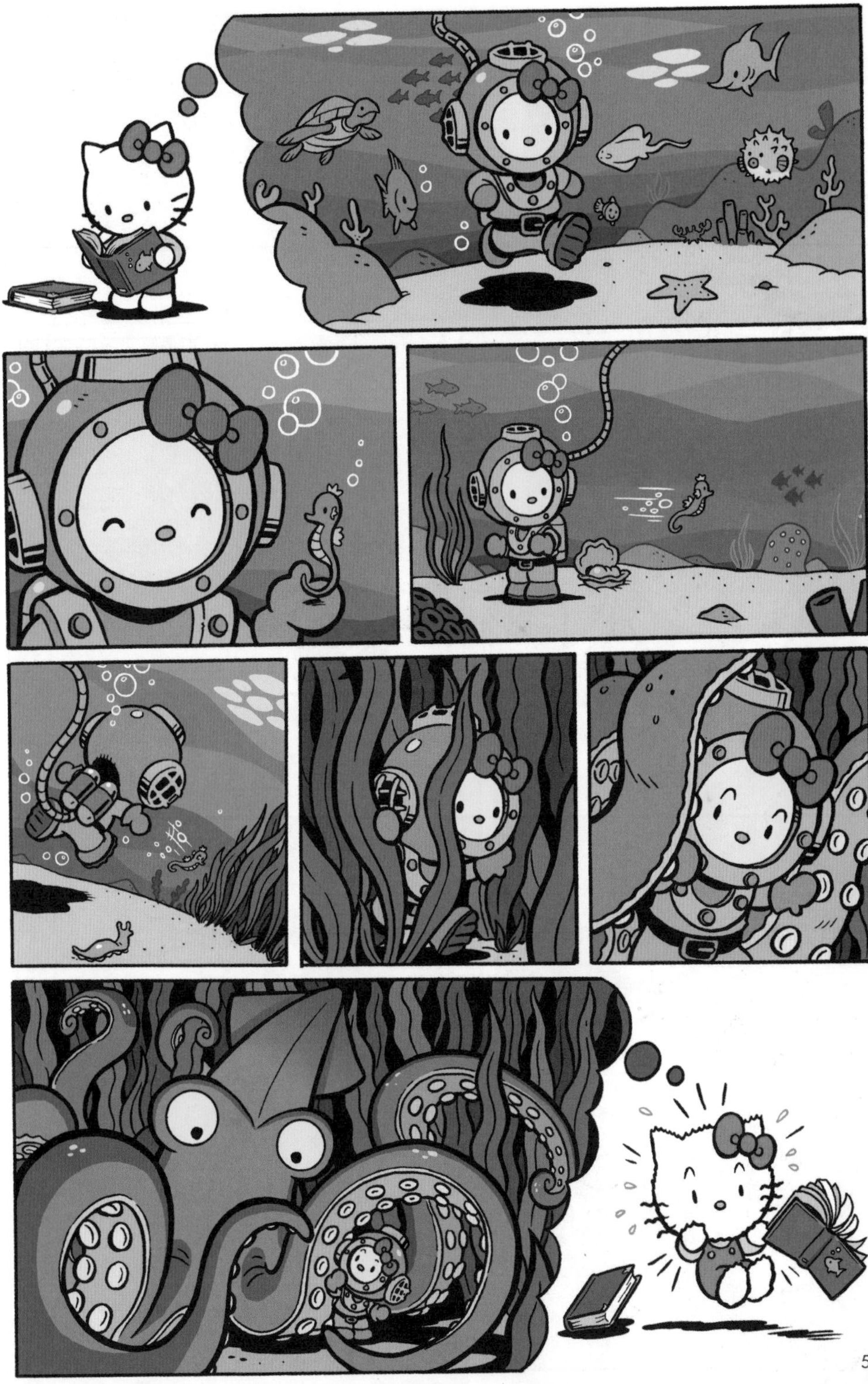

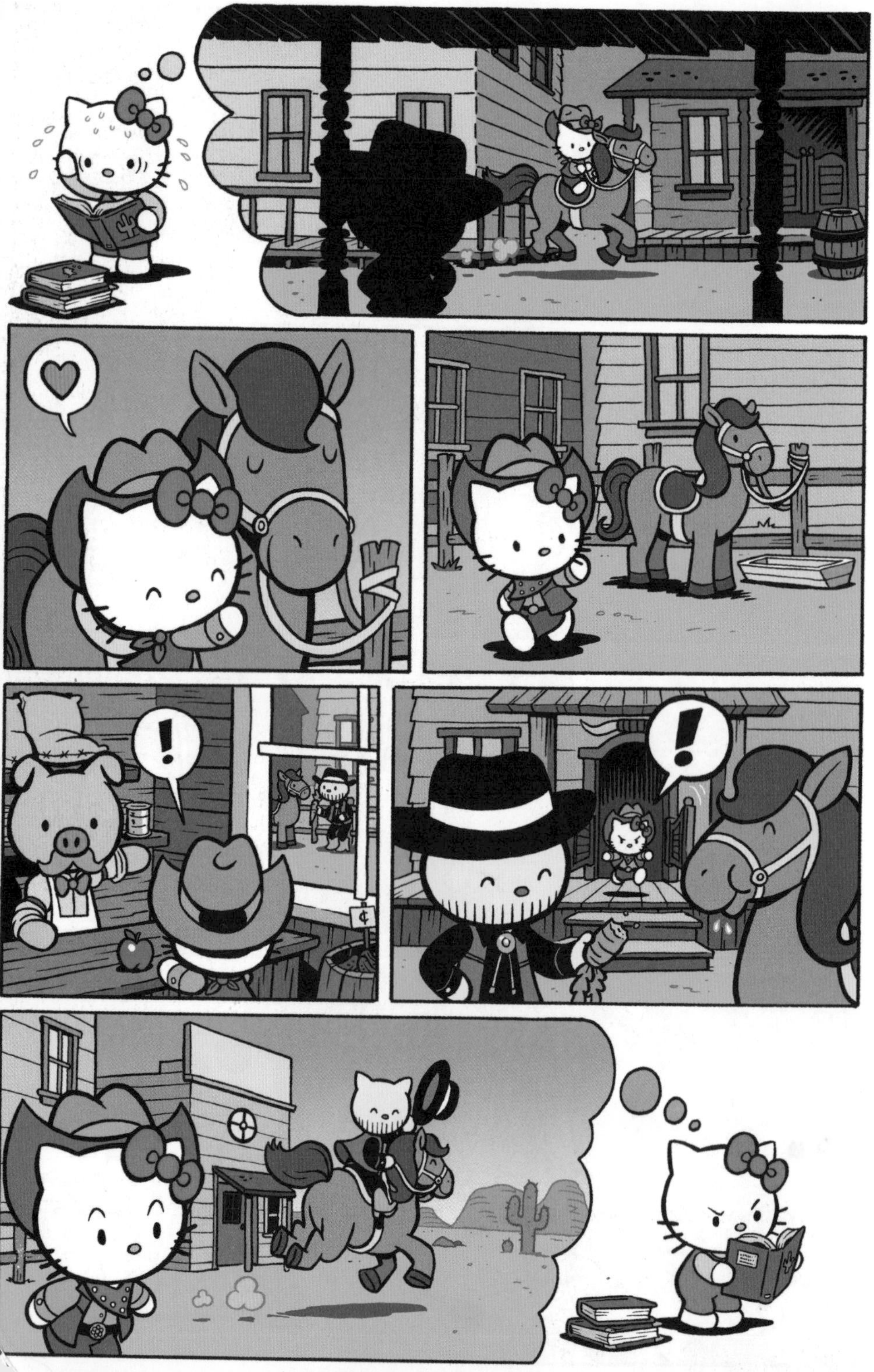
!
¢
!

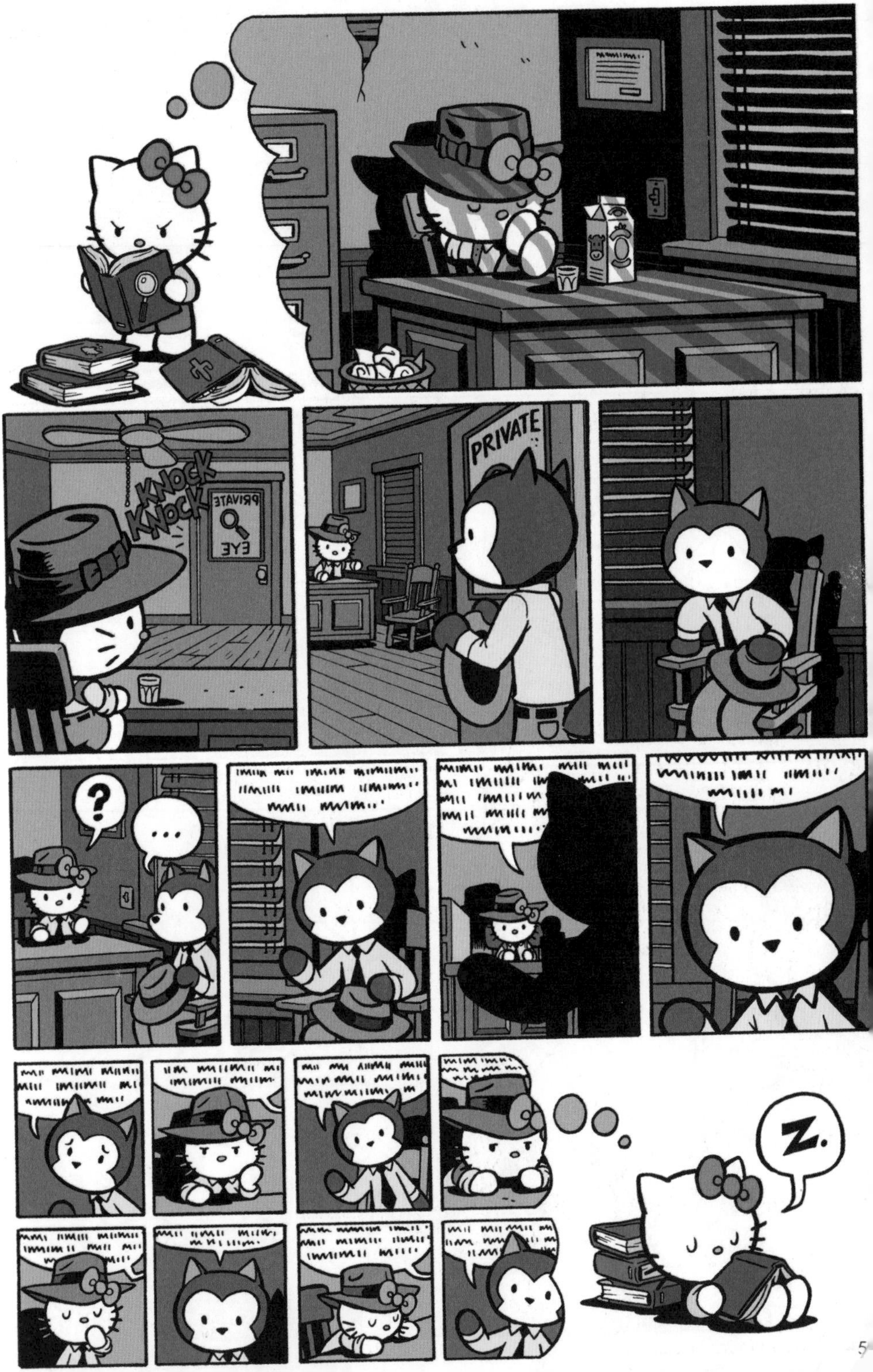
KNOCK KNOCK
PRIVATE EYE
PRIVATE
?
...
Z.

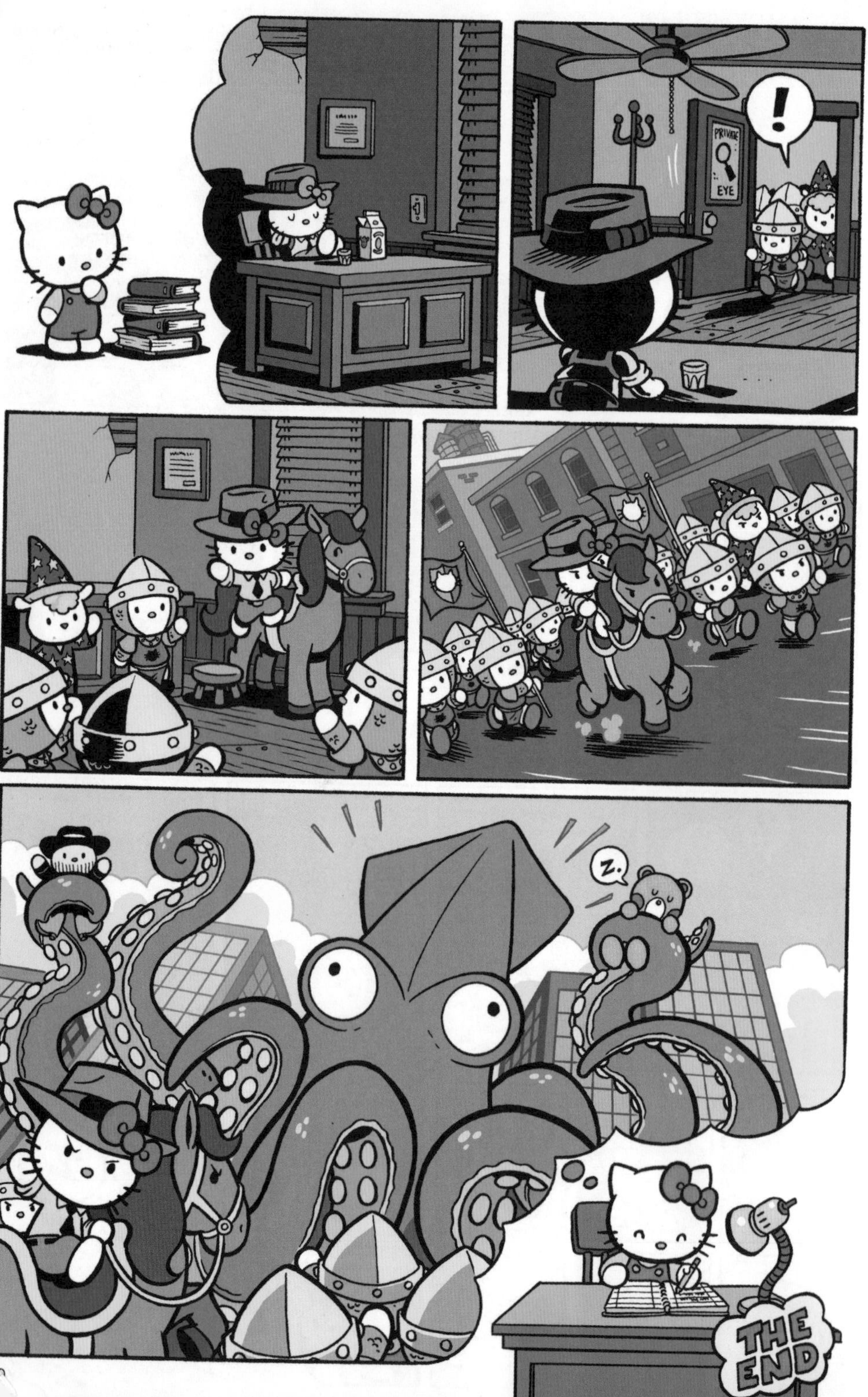
!
PRIVATE EYE
Z.
THE END

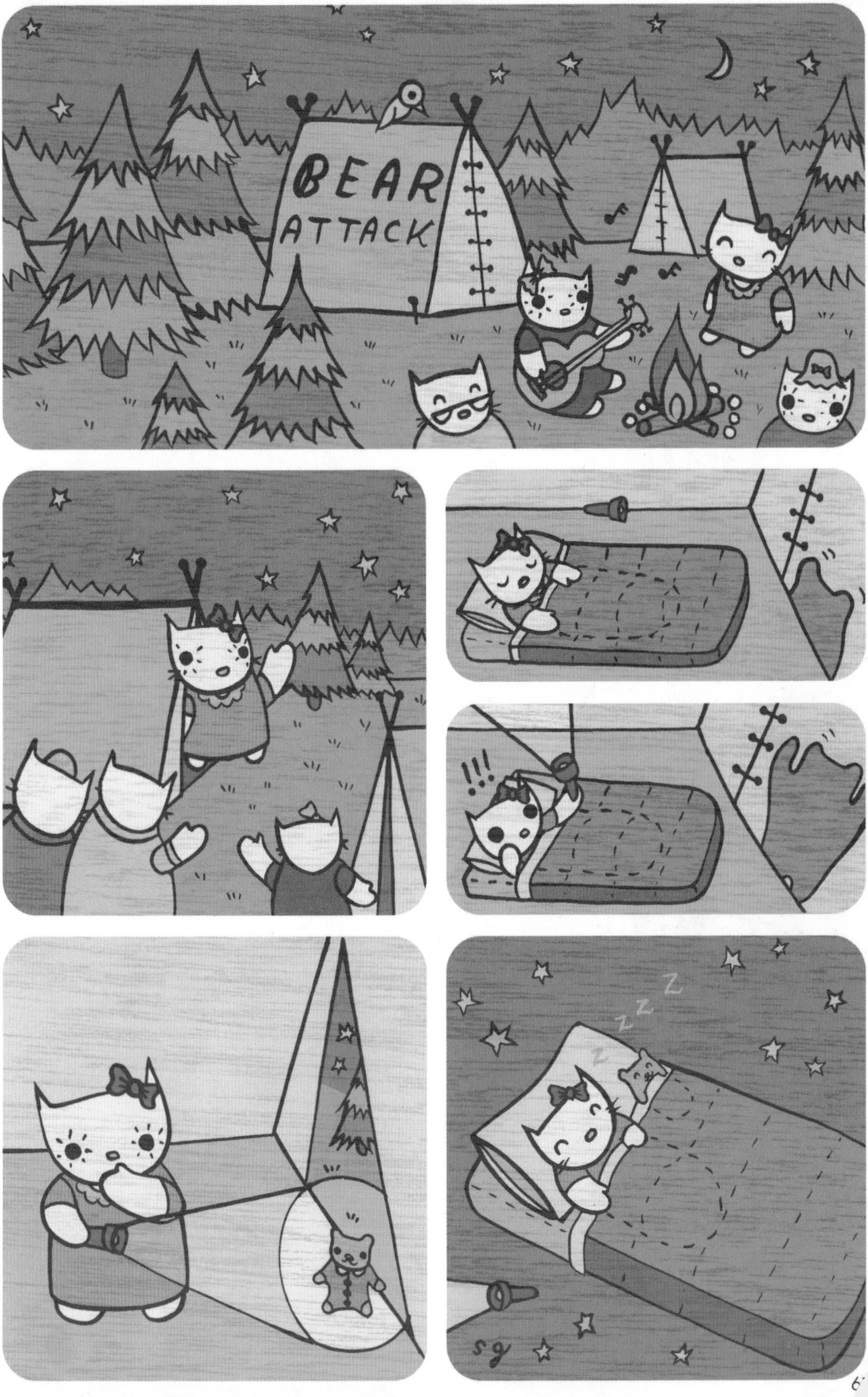
BEAR
ATTACK
!!!
Z Z Z Z
sg

Creators

Jacob Chabot is a New York City-based cartoonist and illustrator. His comics have appeared in publications such as *Nickelodeon Magazine*, *Mad Magazine*, *Spongebob Comics*, and various Marvel titles. He also illustrated *Voltron Force: Shelter from the Storm* and *Voltron Force: True Colors* for VIZ Media. His comic *The Mighty Skullboy Army* is published through Dark Horse and in 2008 was nominated for an Eisner Award for Best Book for Teens.

Jorge Monlongo makes comic books, editorial and children's illustrations and video game designs and paints on canvas and walls. He combines traditional and digital techniques to create worlds in beautiful colors that usually hide terrible secrets. You can see his works in the press (*El Pais*, *Muy interesante*, *Rolling Stone*) and read his comic book series, *Mameshiba*, published by VIZ Media in the USA.

Susie Ghahremani wields a tiny paintbrush with a steady hand. In addition to illustrating for commercial and editorial clients such as Chronicle Books, Bloomsbury USA, Bank of America, Target, T-Mobile, and *The New York Times*, she crafts and develops her own line of stationery and gift items under the pseudonym Boygirlparty®. She's an award-winning artist who exhibits her paintings internationally and has illustrated her first picture book, *What Will Hatch?*, written by Jennifer Ward. Susie lives in sunny San Diego, California, with her husband and zillions of pets.

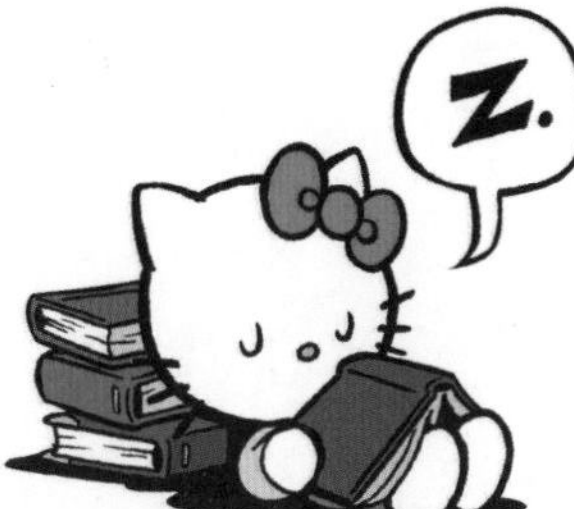
Z.

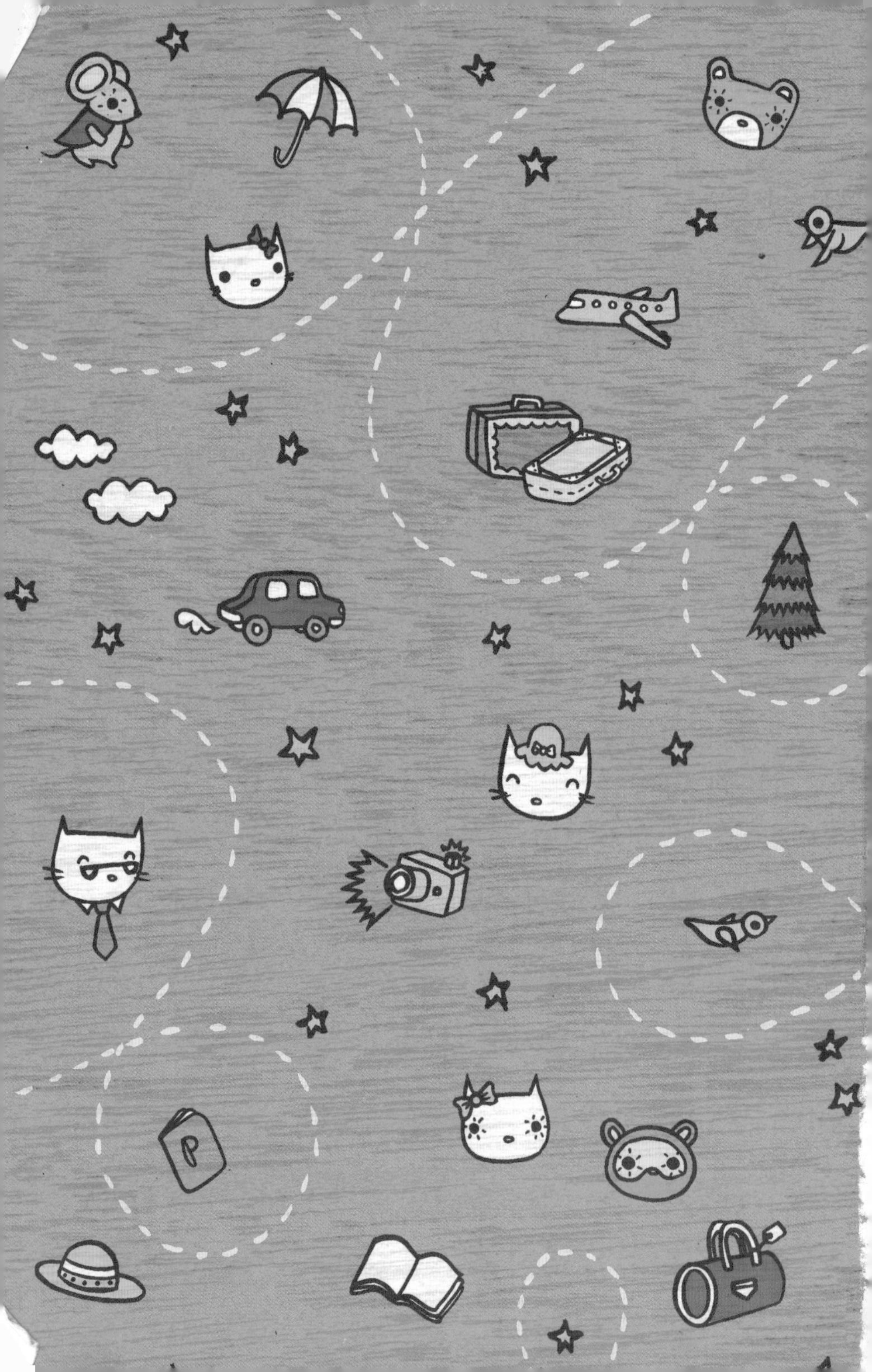